ALSO BY CARMEN ROSALES

The Prey Series

Thirst

Lust

Appetite

Forgive Me For I Have Sinned

Forbidden Flesh

Hillside Kings Series

Hidden Scars

Hidden Lies

Hidden Secrets

Hidden Truths

Cartel Kings Book One

Duets

Giselle

Briana

He Loves Me Not

He Loves Me

Standalone

Like A Moth To A Flame

Delilah Croww Books

Whispers in the Dark

Circle of Freaks

ENVY

CARMEN ROSALES

PREFACE

Sold into slavery to a depraved man, I was meant to serve.
To obey. To deceive.
But when the Order uncovered his secret, they gave him a
choice: send me to Kenyan University, or he'd lose his
claim over me.
At the university, I wasn't just a student. I was Prey—a
label that marked me as less than human in their brutal
hierarchy. Unlike others marked the same, though, I
couldn't be hunted. I couldn't be caught. Everyone
thought they knew me—until my lies unraveled.
Branded a liar, I became an outcast in a world where
power thrives on manipulation and deception.
But then came him.
Garret Nox.
Manipulative. Vicious. Addictive. He is a predator
disguised as perfection, a psychopath hiding behind the
mask of a golden boy. Despite the warnings to avoid him,
his fixation on me is unavoidable.
They say envy consumes everything it touches. And
Garret? He's the embodiment of it.
Now, I'm caught in a dangerous game where the envious
don't just covet the Prey—they destroy them. The only
question left is: Will I survive his obsession?

Erotic Quill Publishing, LLC
3020 NE 41st Terrace STE 9 #243
Homestead, Fl. 33033

www.carmenrosales.com
Rights carmen@carmenrosales.com

AUTHORS NOTE

Dear Reader,

A short list of triggers include depression, death, suicide, acts of violence, and acts of bullying. Please note: This book may be too dark for some readers and caution is advised.

If you or know anyone you know that is suffering from mental health and needs help. Please call National Suicide Prevention Lifeline.

CHAPTER ONE

THE VOICES NEVER STOP.

The whispers. The lies.

Conversations float around the room as I sit here like I'm nothing. Because to them, I am nothing. I'm something you buy. To use. To discard.

I was bought and paid for because no one wanted me. They still don't. They never will. Especially the one who owns me.

John.

He doesn't see me as human. To him, I'm his sick fetish in the flesh—the kind of men like him try to hide, but always fail. Because secrets always come to light.

"She needs to go, John," David, his lawyer says, pacing the room.

"You can't have her go anywhere else," Mary says. Her ice-blue gaze burning into me like acid.

Mary.

If there is one person in this world who would love to see me gone or dead, it would be her. When she married John, she learned the truth. That her husband's interest in her was never real. That she was nothing but a public mask to cover his depravity.

And that I exist.

At first, I thought she would help me. Free me.

But instead, she hates me. More than anything.

She never lets me forget how much. Sometimes, I wish she would end it and be done with me. It would be better than what John does behind closed doors. It would be better than the pain.

I tried before.

Cutting. Hanging. Even stepping out of a moving car.

Each attempt—stolen from me.

John made sure I didn't succeed. And each time I fail, he makes sure he makes me pay in ways no human should inflict on another.

After a while, hope seems like something I should have abandoned a long time ago.

Suicide was the only answer plaguing my mind ever since John appeared in my life: How could I end it? What would be the quickest way I could die so it could all go away? For the voices to stop.

The desire to kill oneself is not as hard as some people think—not when you don't have a choice. It's not what I really want, but it's the only thing I can think about when I want the pain to stop. Wanting to die is a choice for some because there isn't a better option when living is too painful. For others, it's an imbalance in their brain for which they don't have a cure. But not for me. For me, it's freedom from this invisible cage.

"I know," John says, exhaling through his nose. "She will also get the care she needs there, but…"

"You don't want her running off with someone or getting any ideas if she goes to Ohio State, do you?" Mary tilts her head, voice dripping with concern like she gives a shit.

John presses his lips together.

"If she doesn't go," Mary continues, "people will start asking questions. The board members are not asking. The media isn't helping." She sighs. "We gave a statement. We said we adopted her internationally. It's what they wanted to hear."

I remain still.

Mary keeps rattling off excuses and lies. I'm trying to understand what they want to do with me. Where will they hide me next?

"Kenyan University will not accept homeschooled students," Mary says, "because she doesn't have any record of academic achievements. She doesn't qualify for a scholarship anywhere else. She doesn't have the test scores or the grades."

"But she won't be like the others," John retorts, leaning back on his wooden office desk and staring straight at me.

I can still taste the tang from the maple syrup on my tongue from this morning, making me want to vomit all over his designer shoes.

"She'll have to stay in a dorm when she starts her freshman year. She doesn't have lineage," Davids says like a warning. "John?" David voice cuts through the room, hesitant.

John's gaze darts to his lawyer.

David's gaze dips to my legs waiting for him to respond.

My fingers itch to pull the hem of my dress down my thighs like a rash needing to be scratched, but I know better.

I don't move.

I don't react.

I stare straight ahead, wishing I wasn't in the room. To them, my voice, my thoughts, or feelings don't matter. To John, it's my body that holds value. It's what I wear. How I move. How I obey.

"David, are you sure Rose can go through with what we discussed?" John asks, his voice oddly light.

David's cold stare locks onto me. The massage clear. I don't have a fucking choice. "She will."

"Look, I know how you feel about Rose going to Kenyan Prep High School as a senior, but it's the only way she can get into Kenyan University without raising questions and to comply with what the board wants," Mary says. "She will be in good hands,"

My stomach twists. But I don't know if I'm being sent somewhere worse. For the first time, I might be finally leaving this house.

"There is one subject we haven't covered," David says.

My ears perk up.

"And what is that, David?" Mary asks, sounding bored.

David's gaze flicks to me. Then to John. Then, finally, to Mary. "Your son."

John's expression hardens, filled with warning—a warning I don't understand because I've never met Mary's son.

I've heard snippets here and there. I've only heard his name a couple of times. Apparently, he's trouble. The bad kind. The kind that pisses people with money off.

Mary was a widow before she married John and has an older son, whom he is not quite fond of.

Garret.

Mary slowly crosses the room. She bends down until she is eye level with me. "That won't be an issue, gentlemen," she says, her tone full of hatred slicing through me.

I know not to speak. Not until John says I can. Mary knows this. Garret doesn't know I exist, but obviously, when I arrive at Kenyan, he will.

She lets the silence stretch before she leans in, her

perfume filling my lungs like poison. "My son Garret is off-limits to you," she whispers. Her fingers tighten around my wrist. "If you so much as touch my son, I will have you raped and beaten."

John steps forward once she pulls away. "If you so much as allow another man to touch you, I will bring you back here myself." His breath is hot against my skin. I go still. My stomach turns. The sound of his zipper causes my lungs to seize.

I close my eyes. Then softly—loud enough for him to hear—I whisper the only words I'm allowed. "Yes, master."

"Good girl." He undoes his belt, the brass buckle clanking like a bell. "Mary, you can watch or you can leave. The choice is yours."

Her heels thud on the wood floor. Her Chanel No. 5 perfume wafts away like a breeze, replaced by the scent of leather and sandalwood—two scents I hate, splitting my stomach in half.

The sound of the door swinging open makes my heart thud rapidly as she leaves. "Make sure she understands, John. It's bad enough I've had to deal with her filth in my house." The door slams shut with a thud.

"Open your eyes, Rose," John demands. My eyes open, and they focus on his hand fisting his cock, the tip inches from my nose making me gag.

David watches every second, his arms crossed and his cock tenting his black slacks. *Pig. All of them.*

"Open for me," John demands.

"Yes, master," I whisper reluctantly.

"You won't need another man when your mouth is full of me." He grips my hair savagely, tilting my head back, and shoves his cock into my mouth to the back of my throat, eliciting a choking sound. I try to suppress my gag reflex, trying to blank out the stinging pain.

My eyes roll back in my head as my lungs fight for air. Pain smothers my shame as I refuse to let him see my tears, but they slide down my cheeks anyway.

"That's it," he says, thrusting in my mouth. "That's my girl. Take it. You were born to serve me and only me. Touch another man, and I'll fuck your bleeding corpse."

I'm choking, but he doesn't care. The inside of my throat is on fire. My skull throbs in pain while his nails dig into my scalp. He won't stop until I pass out or he comes.

There are times I've woken up naked on the floor, and he's fucking me. There is no question he is good on his threats. John is evil—a pedophile of the worst kind. Sick and twisted and this time won't be different.

CHAPTER TWO

Present Day

"ARE you sure you're not my sister?" Melody's voice is calm, but I hear it—the crack beneath her words, the disappointment behind the question.

I know her mind is fragile, but when she's in this state —the one where she remembers—it's better to give her the truth. "I'm sure."

It's the only thing I can admit.

She exhales sharply. "Well, shit." A loud sigh escapes her. "How did you know?"

I shrug, not wanting to say the words. Valen must have found out. Maybe it was David—the biggest fucking liar the devil created. Who also happens to know Garret. A little detail John and Mary left out.

It was all part of the plan. A way to make me fit in. A way to get me close enough to them. I had to go along with it. It's not like I ever had a choice.

"Do you know who—"

"My parents are?" I finish for her. I let out a puff of air, wishing I had an answer. "All I remember is being in a place with a lot of kids. I was about ten."

I leave out the part where all the girls—including me— were drugged inside a room in some building in the middle of nowhere. "All I know is that John Strauss adopted me."

"Garret's stepfather," Melody mutters.

Garret.

Mary's spoiled son. The one who inherited a fortune and lives like a crowned prince, fucking his way through Kenyan university. A mask of perfection. He parties as hard as he deceives. Drugs, sex, and power.

But I saw it the moment I met him. The truth beneath the mask. He is not what they think.

He is undeniably beautiful: dark hair, chiseled jaw, and a cocky attitude. Melody warned me a couple of times that he didn't take anything or anyone seriously. He's the life of the party. And at one time, girls didn't go for him because he wasn't popular but now, he's all they want.

There's a darkness inside him that rivals John's. And once he learned who I was—that I belonged to John Strauss—his mask slipped. The air in the room felt like it was sucked out and replaced with hate. Unadulterated hate. I was John and Mary's dirty little secret, and I'm not to be trusted. We were enemies.

"We all graduated," Melody says to Valen as if I'm not in the room. As if I don't exist.

"I know." Valen's tone is careful, trying to avoid looking at me while softening his gaze on Melody. Nostalgia hitting me hard in the ribs. I wish someone looked at me that way. It's possessive—but the good kind. The kind you wish for.

I shift on their couch, letting the familiar feeling of being unwanted settle in my chest.

I'm a liar.

An outcast.

Prey without protection.

It's what she's telling me without saying it. I'm not her problem. I have no ties to her or her friends.

"Do you know what that means, Rose?" Her gaze locks on mine.

"I do." My voice barely makes it out.

Valen stiffens. "I think it's best you leave." His tone final.

He doesn't know why I lied, but I'm not his problem for him to give a shit. His priority is Melody, as it should be.

At first, I didn't see how all this would affect me. How it would affect anyone. I've never had friends or felt love from anyone.

But this is what John wanted—a way to sever any hope that I would find someone who would care about me. But most of all, he wanted to make sure I wasn't protected by the sons of Kenyan.

I get up and reach for my sweater. The only one I own. A cheap contrast to the designer one Melody wears. It says Kenyan University—the same one they give all Prey. A way to distinguish us from the rest. I'm sure Melody got one too. And I'm sure Valen never let her wear it. Because Melody is not me.

She's the opposite of everything I represent.

I was bought.

She was chosen.

I am hated.

She is loved.

I want to die.

She wants to live.

I am nothing.

She is everything.

"I'm sorry," I say softly. My stomach sinks when she looks away.

The front door shuts behind me like the final nail in my coffin.

The sun is painted in twilight when I pull my phone. I type out the message as instructed.

Rose: It's done.

M: Good.

A voice cuts through the silence. "Do you need a ride?"

I jolt. The phone almost slips from my fingers. I turn. Azriel leans against a pillar, taking a slow drag from his vape.

"You scared me," I exhale.

He tucks the vape into his pocket and steps forward. The setting sun bleeds against his face, painting in molten gold. "I didn't mean to."

His face has changed. The acne gone, thanks to Melody. And thanks to his brother, he's not as quiet anymore. He's nicer. Handsome, too. Lean. Tall. Strong jaw. Dark brown eyes. Tattoos on his neck that weren't there before.

"It's fine." I clear my throat, knowing I need to go. "I gotta go."

"How do you plan on doing that?"

I blink. "Excuse me?"

He arches a brow and points to the driveway.

"How are you gonna leave? You don't have a car."

"I was going to order a ride." I leave out the part that I don't have money to order one. I was about to ask John to add funds to my account.

The pity in his eyes is sharp. "No need. I'll drive you." He's just being nice. Or maybe, he's like the rest of them.

"That's okay."

"Why not?" His tone shifts. His eyes are pools of chocolate, like he's morphing into someone I should be afraid of.

I clutch my phone tighter. "I don't think your family would approve." His eyes drop to my hand, then back to my face.

"Honestly," he muses.

I think they want me gone as soon as possible."

"Then me taking you would be the logical choice. Why make things more difficult when I could just drop you off?"

He has a point, but I'm unsure of his motives. Is it out of pity? Does he want me gone?

A shiver runs down my spine. Maybe they want me gone, like dead?

Maybe, I'll finally get my wish. A way to fuck over John.

It's what prompts me to agree. "You're right. that does make sense."

He walks to his blacked-out truck, parked on the far side of the driveway like a hearse waiting for me to get in. The twilight sky darkens everything around us like a blanket revealing the stars.

"I'm not like my brother or the others," he says.

I don't say anything as I stare straight ahead. My opinion doesn't matter.

"I'm sure you had a reason to lie. It's none of my business to ask you why you did, but you do understand that Melody is like a sister to me, and whoever hurts her..."

I blink back tears. The reminder of what I've done feels like splinters pricking my skin. I still don't answer. I don't look at him. I don't even say thank you when he stops in front of my dorm because I know he's too good inside to do it and I'm not worth it.

"Rose?" He clears his throat. School starts on Monday—"

My phone vibrates in my lap, interrupting what he was about to say. The screen lights up with the notification. Azriel's voice fades into the background as pure panic sets in when I read the message.

M: Get out of the truck.

I swallow thickly, my throat is like sandpaper. The mistake of getting in his truck hits me like a bug on a windshield.

He's always watching. I shouldn't have involved Azriel like this.

My phone buzzes again.

M: Now.

I close my eyes and grip my phone. I pull the handle, hoping for a split second that Azriel would drive off, but I know he won't.

I can feel his gaze burning like the sun. "Rose, are you okay?"

I push the door open, jump out, and run toward the doors to get inside the building. My lungs burn. My heart pounds in my ears, drowning out Azriel's voice follows me. "Rose!"

I open the door and run down the hallway. My thighs burn. My vision narrows like I'm in a tunnel. A hand clamps over my mouth. The scent of ether and chemicals fills my lungs.

I kick.

I thrash.

"Come on," a man's voice says.

I can't see behind me. I'm dragged to the back exit. I try

to kick, but the arm wrapped around me is too strong. I feel the air shift. I'm outside.

A black SUV skids to a stop. The back passenger door is flung open. I'm pulled inside. All the air whooshes out of my lungs when something hard hits my head. A crack of pain explodes in my head and darkness swallows me whole.

CHAPTER THREE

MY EYES FLUTTER OPEN, and I sputter from the cold water. Shocks me back from the abyss. The pain in my wrists, The bite of the restraints. A red light.

John's voice slithers through my mind— a never-ending nightmare. His hot heavy breath against my skin. The weight of him. This time, he drugged me. I remember slipping in and out—wishing I'd stay in the dark. But the cold water keeps pulling me back.

The spray stings, electric against my skin, and I gasp as reality slams into me. Off-white tiles. Metal brackets from a stall. Fluorescent lights. I'm back in my dorm's shower.

Something warm pools between my thighs causing my muscles to lock up. For split second, terror seizes me but then I realize I'm peeing. The drugs are wearing off. I wiggle my fingers, testing. Movement comes slowly. I press my palms against the cold tiles, trying to drag myself away from the water. A sharp spike of nausea coils in my gut.

A puff of air escapes my throat. Pain erupts through my ribs. I sob. Fuck. I try again, but my body doesn't move. It's all in my head.

I stare at the same crack in the tile, my vision blurring in and out. A frustrated moan rumbles from my lips when I realize I haven't moved an inch. It's all in my head. Then—

Thud.

Thud.

Thud.

Footsteps.

My eyes roll back. *Someone is coming.*

I try to call for help, but my throat is raw.

I try again. Nothing.

The fluorescent lights swirl, tilting beneath. And then, I float. Something warm presses against me. Heat melts into my frozen skin, chasing the cold away. For the first time, I don't fight it.

If this is death, I'm home. Because living is my true hell.

———

I'm weightless, suspended on a cloud. For a second, I savor the quiet. I count to five. Then open my eyes. Two black orbs stare back. Blink. Something wet, leathery, breathing. It blinks again. Metal. Spikes. A growl. My pulse spikes. It's a fucking dog. A big, black dog. With pointed teeth and bared teeth.

I yelp—my voice hoarse, broken. I bolt upright. Catching the soft black sheets, clutching them to my chest, trimmed in gold. The bed is enormous. And I'm naked.

Where am I?

My head whips around, the room is huge and unfamiliar. Black oak floors. Dark furniture. Monochrome colors carefully placed by design. The windows are covered in heavy drapes. The air smells different. Not like John. Not like the others.

A sharp growl pulls me back. The dog sits in front of the door. A Doberman Pinscher. Large. Watching. Waiting.

I test a slow movement, pausing the growl deepens. Shit. Whose fucking dog is this?

I try again, inch by inch. The Doberman raises its head. I sigh and lean against the headboard, staring at the beast. "Who do you belong to?" I ask.

The dog's ears flick. It watches me without blinking. Minutes pass. My heartbeat slows.

I scan the room—really scan. Ni chains. No cuffs. No red lights. This is not John's house. I would be locked in a small room with a twin bed, not in a room this luxurious. And John would never leave me alone. He would never leave me with a dog either.

Desperation sets in after sitting still for so long. I wonder how long I've been here. The smell of cologne on the sheets doesn't help. It's not one I'm not familiar with. It's how I learned who John let in. Their cologne. Their sweat. Their sickness. I knew which ones were violent, cruel. Which ones would use me the worst.

It's how I could tell what kind of day I was having. It's funny how quickly you tune in to your other senses when you're tortured—raped, hit, slapped. I knew them by their scent when the drugs kicked in and my vision blurred. And this scent isn't his.

A whine snaps me back to the present. The Doberman circles, then sits again. It watches me with the same unreadable expression. I shift lightly. Another growl. I sigh.

"You're trained," I mutter. The growl stops. I raise brow. "You're not attacking me. You're keeping me here." Black eyes shimmer under the dim light of the chrome lamp.

Talking then.

"I never had a pet," I continue, studying it. "Looking at you, I don't think I'm a dog person." He whines, stretches, then stretches its long leg as if I'm about to tell him a story, and he's going to be bored.

I pull the soft black sheet to my nose, causing his head to rise in curiosity. I pause. He does too. I sniff. Wood, floral, and a touch of amber.

Nothing I recognize.

The door opens. My breath hitches. All the oxygen in my lungs rushes out. My fingers fist the sheet. I stare at the last person I expect steps inside.

CHAPTER FOUR

"WHY THE FUCK AM I HERE?" My voice cracks, choked and raw.

Garret snaps his fingers. The dog obeys, slipping out the door.

He tilts his head, black hair falling over his brow, a slow smirk tugging at the corner of his mouth. "I knew you had venom in there somewhere." The smile isn't friendly. It's calculated. "You know"—he crosses his tattooed arms over his chest—"you should be thanking me."

I grip the sheet tighter, the soft fabric the only thing shielding me from him."What do you want from me, Garret?"

The playfulness vanishes. His expression shifts, the light in his gaze flickering from golden boy to something colder.

Darker.

Like a switch flipping, light to dark.

He moves to the side of the bed. I pull away, pressing into the headboard, hating how I cower. But I know evil when I see it. And Garret?

He's worse than evil.

He's deceptive.

A manipulator.

He lets you think you're in control. Lets you believe you've figured him out. When in reality? You were playing his game all along.

"You're clutching that sheet really tight, Rose."

My heart pounds, hammering against my ribs. A slow trickle of sweat slides down my spine.

"I've already seen what I wanted to see."

"Fuck you."

He laughs. A sharp, maniacal chuckle. "Uh, no. I don't fuck dirty cum rags. I like mine clean."

I flinch, but I don't look away. "Then why didn't you leave me where you found me?" I challenge. "Why go through all the trouble?"

His gaze flickers—brief, unreadable. Like a serial killer caught mid-thought. You think the answer he gives you is the truth, but it never is Garret doesn't act without reason. He's been waiting. Watching. Every time I was with Melody and the others.

Evil men like Garret don't operate in chaos. They operate in silence. In the shadows.

He smiles, but his eyes stay cold. "I had to see for myself what the fuss was all about."

His gaze drops—slow, deliberate. Down my chest. Further.

Heat crawls under my skin. Then, hot and cold at the same time.

He didn't touch me. Didn't fuck me.

He just said he didn't. Besides, Garret doesn't need to drug women to have sex. That's not his style. He wants you to know it's happening. Because what he really fucks is your mind.

"And?" I force out.

The corner of his mouth lifts. Not a smile. Something worse. I want to run.

Crawl my way out if I have to. But I can't. I can scream, but no one will hear me. I can fight, but he's stronger. And

I've learned one thing about rich men with power. Running only makes it worse.

Garret leans closer. Bends at the waist until his mouth is inches from my cheek, his breath candy-sweet against my skin. "Take your fingers," he says slowly, "and run them above your slit."

My pulse skitters. His gaze drops to my hand.

"I'm not going to ask twice."

Fucking asshole. He's trying to tell me something, but he wants me to find out his way. The most humiliating way possible.

I hesitate. Then do as he says. My fingers slide beneath the sheet. His gaze stays locked on mine. I expect prickly hair. Rough skin. But it's smooth. Buttery soft. Bare. Shaved. The realization hits me like a freight train. Garret shaved me.

He bathed me.

I haven't had a razor in weeks. And John, he liked it grown out. He said it made me more of a woman. Sick fuck.

But Garret? Garret had a different reason.

I drag in a breath. "Congratulations." My voice drips venom. "You've seen me naked and decided to be a creep, so what now?"

He sits at the edge of the bed. But with him there, it feels small. "For the record," he says, "we both know I'm not a creep." I hate how perfect he is. How beautiful. "I cleaned up my stepfather's cum from your pussy." He pulls the sheet back. And stares at the tattoo on my left shoulder. The numbers. My cattle brand.

His eyes narrow. His tongue drags over his bottom lip. His fingers skim the numbers causing my nipples to go hard. "Does it mean something special, Rose?"

It's the date I was enslaved. Written backward. To some, it's just a set of numbers. To me, it's the day I was destined to die a slow death.

But I don't say that.

I lift my chin. "If you know, you know. It doesn't matter what you think."

"I think what most people in Kenyan think," Garret says, leaning back. "You're a liar. And you're Prey."

My stomach sinks.

"You are fair game," he continues. "On campus, you belong to us."

My blood runs cold. "Us?"

"It's no different than what you like to do with John."

Rage churns inside me. He doesn't know. But it's killing him. And I can't tell him. I lift my chin. "Your mother made it clear to stay the fuck away from her son."

Garret's jaw tics. His mask slips—just slightly.

I snort. "Lucky for her, she never had to worry." I lean forward, mirroring him. "I'd rather fuck a corpse than an entitled prick like you."

I struck a nerve. His gaze darkens. His lips curl. "Spoken like a true whore."

"You shaved me while I was unconscious," I mock, "because deep down, you know I wouldn't give you the time of day."

His smirk vanishes. "I forgot to add," he says slowly, "a drug-addicted whore."

The words cut deep. He leans back, watching me crumble. "You're so disgusting, your pussy stinks."

I swallow the pain. Forcing my tears down.

Garret stands. Grabs a set of clothes from the dresser.

"You figured me all out," I say, voice flat.

He tosses me a sweatshirt and sweatpants. I pull them on, the fabric soft against my skin. They smell like him.

It's a shame. I'll have to burn them.

CHAPTER FIVE

I STARE at the lettuce sticking out of my sandwich, the edges turning brown from sitting out too long.

I haven't touched it. I'm sitting in the far corner of the cafeteria—the only seat far enough from anyone else.

Another twenty minutes until my next class. I keep my gaze down, but I can feel the stares. It's been like this all week. And every time I hear someone bring up Garret—Kenyan's richest student. Senior. Gorgeous. Star of the swim team.I turn and head in the opposite direction.

I don't want friends. There's no such thing when you're Prey. Especially after everyone heard about the fallout between Melody and me. How I'm not in their circle anymore. How I'm adopted but don't have the right bloodline. Why I'm in the dorms instead of a mansion.

The table shakes. Someone just sat down. I should leave before—

"Hey." A male voice.

I pretend I didn't hear.

"Hey." I look up. Intense brown eyes. A grin, the kind that makes his top lip thinner than the bottom. I don't know him. But apparently, he knows me. "You're Rose, right?"

Laughter pulls my attention to the right. A group of seniors. I can tell by the way they carry themselves. Not Prey. Rich. The kind of troubled kids you don't send to Harvard. The kind you send to an Ivy League school built for the one percent. Some say it wasn't built, but found.

I recognize some from Babylon—the off-campus hangout.

The two blondes and one brunette. Their skirts are so short that if they bend an inch, they will reveal what type of panties they're wearing, if at all—fall weather in Ohio be damned.

When the blondes shift, the brunette leans in. Her sultry smile practiced, perfect. She pulls her sweater low, the neckline dipping.

Her breasts push together, aimed at one target.

Garret.

He stares. Not interested. Not disinterested. Just watching. Her lips move, but he barely listens. He tilts his head. Like he's deciding something.

"That's Cassie."

Almost forgot someone was sitting across from me.

"I'm Luke."

I don't respond. Cassie licks her blood-red lips. Garret smiles. Something twists inside me. I don't want him. I hate him. Right?

"They hook up sometimes," Luke says, watching me. "Garret gets around."

My eyes stay locked on him and Cassie. They have chemistry.

Luke shifts. "Do you know Garret?"

I rip my gaze away, meeting his stare. Like he just asked if I'm friends with a celebrity. "No."

Luke lowers his voice. "You like him, don't you?"

I scoff.

"All the girls do."

I shake my head.

"You can't blame them. He's filthy rich. Captain of the

swim team. Good-looking. He's like a walking lottery ticket."

I look him dead in the eye. "Well, I'm not one of them."

Luke searches my face. He's not convinced. But he's not wrong, either.

Garret is tall. Gorgeous. Dangerous. The kind of man who could make a girl lose herself. But I don't want him.

I want freedom. A place to start over. Somewhere where people don't ask questions. Where I can say "no" and it will actually mean something. Where I can be just a woman. Where a man will ask my name, and I can give him one I chose.

Where he'll smile and ask how my day was. He'll never think of me as polluted. His scent won't remind me of something dark and he will never touch me without permission.

"You're not interested in Garret?"

I roll my eyes. "No, I'm not."

Luke leans in. "You like women, then?"

"No."

A pause. "Do you like anyone?"

I exhale. "No."

"So what's it gonna take for you to go out with me?"

There it is. His real reason for sitting here. I push my plate away. "I don't date."

"Are you a virgin?"

I go still. Then I look at him, tilting my head. "Are you?"

Luke chuckles."No. But you already knew that."

I arch a brow. "How observant of you. Are you going to show me a trick?"

He laughs. But it's not funny. "You know what? I like you."

I raise a brow. "How is that? You don't know me."

Luke leans forward. "There's a party this weekend. At Garret's house."

My stomach clenches. The memory of his bed. His sheets. The way he promised to burn them after I touched them. "I don't like parties," I lie.

I've never been to one. Never been asked out, either. Not even in high school. Back then, I was too socially awkward. The only kids I knew were hopped up on drugs, waiting to be sold.

And Luke? He's not asking me out. He has a motive.

He places his forearms on the table, and it's then that I notice his jacket with the Kenyan swim team logo. He's on the swim team with Garret. "Come on," he says. "It'll be fun."

Garret wouldn't want me there. "I wasn't invited."

And I wouldn't want to go.

"I can change that."

I freeze. My eyes widen as Luke turns, calling out. "Hey, Garret."

I stop breathing. Garret's gaze locks onto me. Cassie? Forgotten.

Luke grins. "I wanna bring a friend this weekend."

I wait for Garret's rebuttal. For him to say, "Hell no." For him to humiliate me. But instead—

Garret smiles. Like a Cheshire cat. "Sure," he says, too smooth. "Bring lots of condoms." He lets the words sink in. "And a bathing suit."

How about a knife to cut off your dick?

My stomach churns. Garret is inviting me. Not because he wants me there. But because he wants me to see. Sex. Money. Drugs. His world. And I just walked right into it.

———

Friday arrives, and I have no intention of showing up at Garret's party. Invited or not, he'd have to kidnap me to get me there.

John owns my weekends and after that, they consist of recuperating. Of trying to piece together what happened the last time he forced me to do whatever he wanted. Half the time, I don't remember. The drugs ensure that. Except when it's just John and me. Then, he prefers me sober. He wants me to remember him. And only him.

Those nights are the worst. When he calls me his good girl. When he pets me after he's done. When he whispers how he loves me. Those are the nights I cry the hardest in my sleep. If it were possible, I'd take a scalpel and scrape every trace of him from my mind.

I walk into the library, trying to forget the weekend is almost here. The girl behind the desk looks up.

"Hi, I'm interested in signing up for tutoring."

She nods and moves around the desk, looking for something. I take the moment to scan the library. It reminds me of a cathedral, except instead of saints and angels, gargoyles perch on the tops of shelves. I inhale deeply. Books. Old wood. Ink. A scent so unlike John's house.

I've been meaning to check some out. To get better.

I struggle in class. Because I was never homeschooled. John and Mary lied. I can barely spell, write, or solve equations. John must have paid off the teachers because my grades were low.

I'm here because I need a tutor. If I don't keep up, Kenyan will kick me out.

And I'll end up back in John's house.

She places a clipboard on the counter. "Here you go."

I scan the names. The only available tutor is A.

"Who's A?"

She shrugs. "Most tutors are hybrid students. This one just goes by A, I guess."

I didn't even know Kenyan had hybrids. Doesn't matter. I write my name, circle a time, and push the clipboard back.

"You're all set," she says. "Tutoring is at the table behind the computers. If you're ten minutes late, you forfeit your time. Three no-shows, and you're out for the semester."

"Got it. Thanks."

I drift toward the literature section. I need a book on the Renaissance era for history class. I scan the shelves, fingers tracing the spines. I pull a book when—

Thump.

A grunt. I freeze. Heavy breathing.

Slowly, I move to the next aisle. My stomach drops.

Muscles taut as a rope as a strong arm braces against the top shelf.

Below him—

Cassie. Her mouth stretched wide, lips stained red, struggling to take him in. She gags. Not in protest but with determination.

Garret thrusts harder, a silver flash catching the light on his watch.

She whimpers. He grips her hair. "Shh..." The command is dark.

His eyes flick to mine. My stomach knots. His gaze doesn't waver.

Cassie follows his line of sight, noticing me. Her face flames with humiliation. Garret doesn't look away. He doesn't stop. But I can't look away either. I should run and pretend I didn't see. But I stand there, book clutched to my chest. Hating that I'm watching. Hating that I'm curious.

Garret's lip curls slightly. Like he knows. Like he's inviting me deeper. He grips her hair harder. "Go."

Cassie stumbles back, wiping her lips. Her glare burns into me before she leaves. I should go too. But—

His hand moves faster, still gripping himself. He steps closer. I step back.

A silent game. A slow, calculated chase. My back hits the bookshelf. He stops, towering over me. The light from the window casts a halo over his dark hair. Like an angel descending. But he's no angel. He's a demon. A predator. And I am prey.

"Garret…" His name escapes my lips like a plea.

He doesn't stop. His fingers move faster. "You like watching, Rose."

My fingers tremble. The book nearly slips from my grasp. A book on love.

He sees the title. His smirk widens. "You're wishing for love?" His breath fans my lips. "For someone to read you sonnets and poems?"

He's mocking me. But his eyes are dark. Wanting.

His forehead presses against mine. The pressure sends tiny pricks down my spine. I should push him away. But I can't.

He smells different. Not like John. Not like any of the men before.

The scent of his skin mixed with cologne envelops me. His forehead pushes against mine, and the pressure sends tiny pricks across my skin. His breath teases my lips, but I'll never kiss him,

"Have you ever wanted something so badly, Rose?"

The words are a prayer, a curse. I clench my hands. The book bites into my palms. "Yes," I whisper.

I won't tell him it's death.

His breath shudders. He licks his lips. "Fuck." His jaw tightens. His body shakes. His forehead rolls against mine. "I'm going to come, Rose."

The pupils in his black eyes expand. A surge of heat. Then—

His cum. I freeze. Hot liquid hits my hand.

My book.

My sweater.

He wipes the tip of his cock on my hand. Tucks himself away. Grips my chin. His cum-stained fingers digging into my skin. "I think you should get yourself cleaned up." His voice is smug, wicked.

I shove him away. "You're disgusting."

He steps forward. "I think we've established how we feel about each other. It looked like you wanted a front-row seat; I gave it to you."

I push him away, trying to wipe my hands on his black sweater, feeling the hard wall of muscles as he steps back to let me pass. "You're an asshole."

"At least I'm not a liar." I walk down the aisle to the back exit. "Don't come to my party and stay away from my friends. It's your only warning."

I push the door and run outside, not caring if I didn't check out the book. It's not like I could hand it to the girl sitting in the front, covered in his cum.

I finally make it to my dorm building with tears streaming down my face. When I reach the bathroom sink, I assess the mess on my hands and my sweater. It's everywhere. He's everywhere.

I scrub my hands and face raw, but it's like he's

embedded in the pores of my skin. The musky scent of his cum mixed with cologne. He doesn't smell like smelly sex or spit.

I'm repulsed with myself for not wanting to gag; for not finding it disgusting. I look up and catch my reflection in the mirror, my eyes are puffy from crying. My cheeks are red and splotchy. I hate myself for not running sooner, for not screaming for help when he caged me.

"I'm sick," I tell myself.

How could I like the smell of his cum or his skin? Why do I still crave his kiss?

CHAPTER SIX

I SCRUB MY SKIN RAW, trying to erase Garret's last words. A warning. A threat.

A reminder to stay away. The words replay in my mind like a catchy hook from a song.

I never showed up at his party. He wanted to scare me off. It worked.

After cleaning the library book as best I can, I sit cross-legged on my bed.

The dorm room is silent. I glance at my phone. 2:00 a.m.

I flip through the book. Sonnets. Plays. I try to read, but as always—

I struggle.

The words blur together. I attempt to read aloud. But I sound horrible.

It reminds me of that day in high school. The teacher called on me to read.

I tried. I stumbled. She made a face and told me to stop. That was the day I realized I couldn't read at the same level as the others. I couldn't multiply or spell.

I was useless.

John wanted it that way. Dependent on him. A girl with no future. He ensured I would never escape.

I flip the page and try again. Tears pool in my eyes. The words won't stick. I can't read a full sentence without stumbling.

I slam the book shut. A sob rattles from my chest.

Knock. Knock.

I freeze. A slip of paper slides beneath my door.

I wipe my face. Heart pounding. I don't move to open the door. What if it's some creep?

I unfold the paper. The ink is delicate. The handwriting elegant. It looks like a poem.

———

I had stayed in my room all weekend, only going to the vending machine for snacks. John gave me twenty dollars a week on a loadable card, claiming it was for tampons and toiletries. It was minimal, but there was nothing I could do. Some people think that if you're adopted by a wealthy family, you're provided for, but not in my case.

John didn't call me the whole weekend, and I was relieved. I hardly slept staring at my phone waiting for the unwanted text to pop up. Trepidation and fear running rapid in my mind.

Maybe he realized he went too far last time and that I needed time to recuperate. I received a text about an upcoming appointment at the campus health center this morning scheduled for 4:00 p.m.—two hours after my scheduled tutoring session with the mysterious person named A. I wouldn't put it past John being behind it and there was no way I could ignore it.

I tried all weekend to improve my reading skills. My phone doesn't have internet access, and I was afraid to walk into the library after the incident with Garret. I had never stolen anything before, and I was petrified. I didn't know what to do, but I needed a tutor for math. Hopefully, no one noticed it was missing.

I walk in ten minutes before my scheduled appointment, relieved that there's a guy at the front desk and that the redhead from last time is nowhere to be found. I tell him I have an appointment with Mr. A.

"He's waiting in the back," he says without looking up from whatever he's reading.

I walk to the designated tutoring table and freeze. An overwhelming urge to run away suddenly washes over me. Garret is sitting at the table where my tutor is supposed to be.

There must be a mistake.

His chiseled jaw and perfect lips move when notices me and asks nonchalant, "Waiting for someone?" His white designer sweater is snug around his arms as he leans back in the wooden chair. His dark hair almost obscures his eyes.

"You're not my tutor," I reply, hoping he isn't because I would be screwed. There's no way I can have him as my tutor.

"No, I'm not." A sense of relief washes over me, steadying the rapid beat of my heart. He points to the chair across from him. "Have a seat, Rose. This will only take a second."

I sit, clutching my bag to my chest as if it will protect me from him. He stares at it with a blank expression. A blush stains my cheeks. The thread at the corners is unraveling, and there are scuff marks and stains on the front even though it's black. I'm sure Garret has never known what it's like to use a bag from a donation box.

He looks up, and I quickly avert my gaze, staring out at the glass windows that overlook the hallway, hoping to catch my tutor to rescue me. As if that would save me from Garret.

Having hung out with Melody a couple of times, I

know he's part of the Order and the Consortium. I know they have the power to eliminate whomever they want. They're killers with money and power, and Garret—he's unhinged. I can see it in his eyes—how he struggles with the darkness inside him.

He reaches for the chair beside and lifts a plastic bag placing it on the table. It's from the café on campus. I didn't know you could bring food into the library, but then again, this is Garret.

"You're no use to us if you don't eat."

The delicious smell wafting from the bag makes my stomach growl, but I push it down, letting his words sink in. "What I eat and when is none of your business."

He leans forward. "That's where you're wrong. As long as you're on campus, you are my business. I think I've made it very clear to you."

"I didn't ask to be here, and I'd appreciate it if you'd leave me the hell alone." I glance at the bag reluctantly. "Take your damn handout with you." I'm seething now, but this is my chance to make my point and push him away. "I don't want anything from you."

"Funny, I didn't see you running for the hills on Friday. You waited until I was finished." He stands and leans over the table, making me feel small as he towers over me. "Eat the fucking food, Rose. Don't make me feed it to you."

Suddenly, I'm lightheaded, and I can't breathe. I can feel my mouth getting thick, as if my tongue is swelling, and soon I won't be able to swallow. Flashes of white and silver. My mouth being stuffed with force. The taste of something runny and cinnamon. My mouth burning. I lean back in my chair violently, my eyes wide.

"What the fuck... Rose." Garret is staring at me, confused.

My skin feels tight.

There's another voice I recognize coming from behind me.

"Rose, what's wrong?"

Azriel.

I shake my head violently, but all I see are flashes of a spoon being force-fed. "Please…" I whisper. I have to calm down and stop this feeling, or they'll know, and then he'll make me pay.

Azriel comes into view, glaring at Garret. "What are you doing, Garret?"

"I should ask the same," he replies icily.

"I'm her tutor."

"I'm fine," I say to no one, but try to sound convincing.

They both swing their gazes to me.

Azriel is the first to speak pulling a chair. "I think it's best we get started."

I'm still at a loss for words. He's A. But how or why? What are the odds? He's a hybrid student. I just never thought of Azriel as being a tutor or having the time to be one with his job.

Garret moves with no intention of taking the food. Instead, he gets in Azriel's face, and they stare at each other, communicating something with their eyes that I can't make out. "Make sure she eats," he drawls disturbingly and walks out.

I stare straight ahead, trying to figure out what just happened. Azriel sits in Garret's chair as if nothing happened. As if this is normal.

"So, you need help with math," he states as he pulls out a notebook, pencil, and calculator.

I open my bag slowly and pull out the book and the notebook with the problems I'm having issues solving.

He pauses, watches me for a few seconds, and then asks what I was expecting him to ask, "What happened the other day?"

I haven't seen or heard from him since John took me, and I didn't expect him to. He made it clear where his loyalty lies. I'm not his problem, and I'm not his friend. I get it.

"Nothing. You gave me a ride," I reply, as if it's perfectly normal.

"I came to your dorm to see if you were alright the next morning, but you didn't answer," he says it almost accusingly, as if I did something wrong or let him down.

"I was probably sleeping," I lie, but I can tell he doesn't believe me and lets it slide.

Who cares at this point if I don't tell him the truth? It's not like he doesn't think I'm a liar, like everyone else. I don't feel guilty anymore.

"I was worried and…"

"Why?" I interrupt.

He pauses as if there's something he wants to say but can't.

"I just am. I can't explain why, but I'm here now, and you need help." He picks up his pencil and takes my assignment.

Time passes quickly as he explains the steps, helping me make sense of the material. I love how easygoing and patient he is when I ask questions. I'm embarrassed to tell him that I struggle with reading the problems.

"There are videos to help you if you get stuck." I look up from the example he wrote down, trying to think of an excuse but coming up empty. "Online."

"I don't have internet on my phone," I finally admit.

Why lie about it when he's helping me not to fail? I

probably should be in remedial classes, but those classes aren't offered.

"Oh," he says, surprised. "There's Wi-Fi. Can't you connect your phone to it?"

"I don't know the password, and I'm not sure my phone is capable."

John gave me a phone when I started school, but it's limited in what it can do. It's the type you see at Walgreens —plain, with a simple screen. It's not the fancy kind I've seen the kids on campus have. I don't even have apps or the capability to listen to music.

"I'll take a look if you don't mind," he says gently. My stomach churns at the thought of him seeing the text messages on my phone. "I mean, if you want."

It feels as though he can read my mind. I want to see if he can help figure it out. I would love to watch videos. Listen to music online but I can't risk it.

"That's okay," I deflect. "I'll figure it out."

"The password is KCAMPUS."

I write it down and then slide the book and notebook into my bag. A piece of paper slips out, and he catches it before it falls. I'm about to reach for it but my stomach drops when he reads it. I'm still wondering who would have slipped it under my door.

"Did you write this?"

I almost want to laugh. I can barely spell at a college level. "No."

He watches me for a few seconds, waiting for me to say more, but I won't tell him that someone slipped it under my door, and I won't admit that I don't understand the meaning behind what it says.

He doesn't push, and it's like a weight has lifted from my chest. "Do you mind if I read it aloud?"

I turn around and scan the library to see if anyone is around, but I find it empty. I really want to know what it means, so I face him and nod.

"It's a sonnet." He clears his throat and begins.

Beneath the moon's cold light, your shadow sleeps,

A ghost spinning the thread of fate.

If you whispered words through purged lips, you chain my eager hands,

And reawaken my cold heart.

Your touch, a thorn that bleeds both sadness and beauty.

A curse I'd endure until the world ends.

Each stolen breath ignites my soul, begging for a poison-laden kiss.

The scent of your skin feeds the darkness within me.

A haven carved from fire and sin.

Though every word you speak is laced with lies,

I'd burn for you and take the blame.

For love that lingers close to ruin's edge,

Is love immortal, bound by the blood that's bled.

The way he reads is perfect. What he read was dark and passionate. Each word knocked on my heart, wanting to get in, but who would write something like that?

Azriel furrows his brow and hands me the lined notebook paper. "Who wrote that?"

I shake my head, looking at the delicately written words. The handwriting is perfect. "I don't know. Is it from a book or something? Maybe someone copied it from a famous writer."

"I don't think so, Rose. I've never heard or read anything like that. Whoever wrote it is…"

I slip the paper delicately into my bag, careful not to ruin it. "Is what?" I press. "What does it mean?"

My stomach twists in anticipation and trepidation. I

don't have a boyfriend. There is no one I can think of that would write something like that but I want to know what it means.

"Well, whoever wrote it is dangerously obsessed."

"I found it and thought it was interesting."

The look in his eyes tells me he is not so sure. "What's with you and Garret?"

I shrug glancing at the bag of food. "I have no idea. "Why?"

"Because he's dangerous," he warns. "I don't want that for you, Rose. I know there is something behind all this and I don't expect you to trust me."

There's no way he knows the truth. "Why do you say that?"

"There always is and remember"—he glances at the bag of food one more time—"there is always someone watching. As for Garret, stay away from him."

CHAPTER SEVEN

I TAKE the elevator to the fourth floor of the student health department and check in with the nurse at the front desk. She says I'm here to see a therapist. I nod as if I understand, but I don't know why John would make me an appointment when I've already lied to the last one about using drugs, having nightmares, or being in a harmful relationship.

I sit in one of the empty chairs closest to the exit. I expected to see more people, but the entire waiting room is deserted. The walls are painted white, like a glass of milk. There are no pictures, no table with magazines, or anything to keep you entertained. There are only two doors and one window: one door for the exit, one for the back rooms, and the window looks out at an elderly woman who appears to be a grandmother.

When my name is called, I walk in and see a woman seated behind a cherry wood desk. Her hands are neatly folded on top, as if she's praying. She wears a red silk blouse and pearls around her neck, her expression serious, as if this is the last thing she wants to do.

"You must be Rose."

"Yes."

She points to the only available chair against the wall. I find it odd that it's so far away from her desk. She doesn't have the customary two chairs facing her desk, as I've seen in other offices.

I sit.

She leans back and doesn't say anything, watching me like I'm an animal she's studying.

"I'm Dr. Wick."

"I'm Rose."

"I think we've established that."

I want to tell her that I was informed I would see a therapist, not a psychiatrist, and that there must be some mistake about why I'm here, but I keep my mouth shut. The last thing I want is for John to find out I'm asking too many questions. There's no such thing as client privacy when it comes to me. Girls like me don't have human rights. We're selected like cattle and then caged.

"I would like to ask you a few questions, and then you can ask me anything you like."

"Okay." The faster I get out of here, the better. I don't trust this woman. She works here and is hired by monsters who run this place. Who knows what her angle with me is?

"There have been reports from dorm security that you have had issues sleeping?"

I blink a few times, convinced there must be some kind of mistake. How could dorm security know anything about my sleeping habits? My door is always closed, and I hardly see security. There are times I didn't even think we had any. I'm still trying to figure out how Garret found me, but he's not someone you can easily ask questions.

"I'm not sure what you mean."

"It's not uncommon. There are students who have nightmares. They scream in their sleep without being aware, and out of concern, other students report it. Security sends it to the school, and then it's forwarded here to the health department. We take these types of reports seriously."

I want to laugh in her face. Does she know what kind of school this is and what they do to the less fortunate trapped here under the pretense of higher education and a promise of a better life? Of course she does. This woman is no better than a demon foaming at the mouth, telling you to screw yourself for her enjoyment. There is no question; this bitch is evil. How dare she call herself a doctor.

I raise a brow. "And? I had a stupid nightmare. What's the big deal?"

"Does this happen often? If so, what do you have nightmares about?"

"I don't remember," I fib.

Of course, I remember John violating me. I remember being force-fed when I refused to eat, raped, humiliated, touched, and drugged. But is she going to do about it?

"Do you have trouble sleeping?"

"You just said I have nightmares."

Is she dumb?

She lets out a frustrated sigh. "How was your childhood?"

She wants to go there. What a bitch.

"I was adopted." I smile sarcastically. "But I'm sure you already knew that."

She smiles back, but the lines don't crease around her eyes. "I did, but I want to see what you remember about your past."

I shrug. "Nothing really. I was adopted when I was a kid."

"Do you remember your parents?" she asks, ready to type my answer on a keyboard.

Pain slices through my chest, wishing I knew, but I don't. I never will. The numbers on my skin told me the truth a long time ago when I pieced it all together.

Girls who had fallen pregnant when they were taken by rich sick fucks would give birth, and those babies were taken to a building in the middle of nowhere with minimal care. The children were undocumented—boys, girls, it doesn't matter.

When they're old enough, they're placed in a room to be drugged and raped. When they're selected to be so-called adopted by a rich family, documents appear, and the child thinks this family is their savior. The father a hero, the mother a saint. But none of it is real. There is no hero. There is no saint. It's just one sick man from hell with a twisted appetite. Then they take you wherever they came from. As for me, they brought me to the states.

"No, I don't."

She asks me how much money I have while I'm on campus and whether my meals are covered. I find her questions a bit odd, but I answer them as best I can. She inquiries about my last physical. I've never had a formal one, so I tell her I don't remember.

She then sends me to the next room to get one and to see a gynecologist for birth control. I should fight her on this but in my case, it isn't a bad thing. I would like to be checked anyway.

A woman with dark brown hair walks in and say her name is Dr. Mullen. I mention that I have an IUD, but says, she will check anyway. Maybe it's because I'm Prey, and this has nothing to do with John but rather the order. Perhaps they require all females to be on some type of contraceptive. I imagine the last thing they want is a bunch of poor kids with rich babies in their stomachs, messing up their bloodlines.

John told me he had one placed when I was unconscious so I wouldn't get pregnant. I felt relieved. I over-heard some girls had their reproductive organs removed.

I'm on the examining table; the woman's head is positioned between my legs, with my heels resting on two metal supports at the end of the table. I feel a tug between my legs. I tilt my head to the side, and watch her as she removes her gloves, but catch a glimpse of bloody fluid on the tips.

"Is there something wrong?" I ask in alarm. Maybe John or someone ruined my insides, or I have some type of disease.

"Everything is fine. The bloody discharge is normal. Your IUD is intact. If you want to regulate your period, it's best to start taking your birth control at the beginning of your cycle."

I want to tell her my cycle is fine, but I'm eager to leave. I'm uncomfortable and want to take a shower. I never expected this visit and don't know who to believe.

I grab my pills from the lady at the front and head toward my dorm building. My stomach drops when my phone goes off. I stare at the screen in horror.

John: Get in the car outside your dorm building.

I look up at the loading zone in front of the building and see a blacked-out Escalade idling.

———

The SUV drops me off in front of the massive entrance of John and Mary's home. I stare at the dark brown double doors like it's a prison and I'm to be sent to the electric chair. I'm not sure why he wants me here during the week. He said weekends, but he skipped last weekend, so maybe he wants to make up for lost time.

The door opens.

The woman who cleans the house doesn't look me in the eyes. She must think I'm disgusting for the things John does and says when she's hovering around. She must think I like it because I don't protest when deep inside, I'm screaming to die.

"Hello, Georgina," I greet, like I do every time.

She turns around, dismissing me like she always does, but I don't care. I hoped maybe one day she would have mercy on me, but I know she won't.

The faint smell of food and coffee makes my stomach churn. My appetite is gone. It's a familiar feeling I've grown accustomed to when I'm in this house. Who would feel hungry when they're a sex slave?

My hands tremble around the torn strap of my book-bag. The deeper I follow her down the long hallway, the louder the voices.

She turns into the dining room with the massive table for fifteen. The cream marble floors with blood-red veins. The grotesque red curtains Mary insisted on draping over the oversized windows.

I hate this house.

I hate the people and the furniture.

"There she is," John says when Georgina moves to the side.

"You didn't tell me, Mother, that my sister was so petite and small," a voice that could only belong to Garret says warmly.

My throat goes dry remembering the taste of his breath. The look on his face when he came. This is a joke. I've never seen Garret set foot in this house. We both know he doesn't see me as a sister.

"Sit," Mary says, coldly watching me like I'm a fly she wants to squash. "I wouldn't call her your sister."

"Well, step-sibling," Garret says with a smile, but I can tell he doesn't find it amusing.

He's wearing a fitted blue sweater that outlines the muscles of his pecs, doing nothing to hide the mural of tattoos on his neck reaching his jawline. I sit across from Garret, next to John, but he isn't having it.

"Why don't you sit next to me so we can get to know each other better?" Garret's gaze slides to John. I can feel the tension radiate between them. John's eyes turn cold, like he wants nothing more than to reach across the massive table and rip his throat out, but Garret doesn't seem fazed. He continues to watch John closely, daring him to object.

Mary smiles triumphantly. And me? I don't know if I should be happy or terrified. One monster or the other. Two of Satan's most powerful demons facing off.

I don't have to be told to move to the other side and take the seat right next to Garret. I sit, and when I inhale the scent of his cologne, my heart starts to beat like a thousand drums in a parade. He moves his hands from the table to his thighs.

My gaze drops to the back of one of his hands with a skull. The veins disappearing under the edge of the sleeve. His clean fingernails. The black nail polish gone, replaced by a clean manicure.

"Have you seen each other on campus?" Mary asks, but I know why she's asking.

"It's obvious I haven't. I've been busy with swimming and..."

"The orgies at those parties you like to throw," John interrupts. "You've heard," Garret replies, but his gaze is scrutinizing him like darts aiming at a bullseye. "You can come if you want to, John. It might be your kind of party."

Mary sucks in a breath.

I swallow, staring at the plate in front of me as Georgina comes beside me and places a piece of meat that smells like dirty socks on my plate. John glances at me and then at Garret, measuring the distance between our chairs. Jealousy and possession drip from his scrutiny like a blazing fire. "Oh, Garret, you're so funny sometimes," Mary chuckles, trying to play it off like it's a joke. Garret tilts back his head and laughs, and it strokes my skin like a caress. How can a laugh be so beautiful yet so dangerous? "I'm fucking with you, John," he says, but I'm not sure John's convinced. This is the first time I've seen John uncomfortable, and it's almost like he's terrified of Garret. "How's school and swimming? Any girlfriends?" Mary asks genuinely, her knife and fork cutting into the meat with precision. I think she cares about Garret and what he thinks, but with who she married, I'm not so sure. I wonder what Garret's father was like. Was he like Garret or John? "I'm beating my time. I think we will go all the way again this year. And her name is Cassie."

The bitter taste of his lie burns, like embers smoldering beneath my ribs, flaring into something foreign. He lied! My stomach clenches. What type of girlfriend lets her boyfriend stay in the library with his cock out with another girl after he dismisses her? "You have to bring her by so we can meet her," Mary gushes, as if he just told her he's getting married. I stare at my plate but feel empty. A waste of space. I don't even know why they bother letting me dine at the table with them. I'm always sent to my room to eat. I don't even know which fork goes with what or why the hell this meat looks like human brains. "Rose?" I look up and meet John's impenetrable gaze. "Eat," he scolds, like I'm a child. I pick up the smallest fork. "Wrong fork," Mary snaps. I drop it like I've been slapped. "I-I'm sorry," I stammer, knowing that John will make me pay for it later. "Mary." But it's not John scolding her; it's Garret. "Give her a break."

"She needs to eat. I've told John she needs to see a doctor for her eating disorder. She's skin and bones." John stares at her like she revealed a secret, but she goes off, knowing John wouldn't disrespect Mary in front of Garret. "He's complained about it before." John turns his focus on me like he's just found out I stole his car as she continues her rant. "She's always had a problem eating since she was little."

"Isss that sooo," Garret says, his voice dripping with sarcasm, each syllable stretched out like a rubber band being pulled. His gaze flicks to me like I'm under a spotlight, the heat of his stare sinking into my bones. His hand is on my thigh, and I swear my breathing stops. "I'll have to make sure she eats then," Garret says, like I'm not even in the room. The heat from his hand spreads like smoke between my thighs. He's so close yet so far. I don't know if I should shove it away or stand. But then, John will know, and he'll make sure it won't happen again. "I give her money for meals, and she's on the meal plan at school," John counters.

"The food at school is disgusting," Garret states. He isn't wrong. The food looks like it's about to expire. It's not meant for the wealthy but for prey. "How much money are you giving her?"

"I beg your pardon?" John says accusingly, like his card

was just declined. "Money?" Garret says, as if he's stupid and hard of hearing. "How much money are you giving her?"

I want to hide under the table.

He could ask me, but Garret knows I won't tell him, and I'm trying to figure out why he suddenly cares. "Enough," John bellows harshly.

"Oh honey, she has everything she needs. I know you always wanted a sister or brother, but…"

"You were too busy taking them out of your stomach so you wouldn't get fat," Garret interjects, taking a sip of his wine.

Mary places her knife down with a clank. "It's not my fault I'm fertile. Your father wanted more children and forbade me to be on any contraceptive. I had a son like he wanted."

"What is so wrong with him wanting more?"

I can feel the anger building, a ten-foot wave wanting to destroy the little fake charade she has going with John. I glance at Garret's plate. He hasn't touched the food either. "I've had enough of you." She's an even bigger monster when she smiles at John as he pours himself another scotch. "John understands. He doesn't want children. Besides, we have Rose."

I want to gag. She's delusional.

Garret throws his napkin onto the meat, the blood bleeding through the white linen. "I gotta go."

"Already?" Mary cries. "But…you just got here."

"I've been here for the past hour, Mary."

"But you haven't eaten your food," she whines.

"It looks like shit."

"It's liver," she explains as if it's a delicacy. "And I'm sure it tastes like shit," he replies dryly. "It is why Rose hasn't touched hers, and I don't blame her." The chair screams when he pushes it back to stand. "I'll drop off Rose."

Why is he defending me?

"That's unnecessary," John argues, placing his scotch glass on the wood with a thud. "I don't think you have a choice," Garret replies scathingly.

Mary glances between John and Garret with wide eyes.

"Let's go, Rose." And he walks out. I don't wait; I grab my bag from the floor and rush out before someone stops me.

The front door slams behind me. I look at the massive driveway and spot him getting into a shiny blacked-out car with two huge letter Rs on the hood. I move to the passenger side and hesitate to pull on the handle. The engine rumbles, and then he's stepping out and walking around the front. He pushes me back gently, pulls the handle, and the smell of rich leather hits me like a caress.

I look up, and his face is hard. Angry. "Get in," he demands.

I slide in, not knowing if this is what I should be doing. My mind and body battle over what is the right thing to do: leave with him or stay and face John. I don't get to decide because Garret is placing the car in drive, pulling out of the driveway. I stare at the screen on his dash, then at his hands and the way they grip the steering wheel. The skull tattoo mocks me with its smile. I sit rigid, afraid to lean back and tarnish his car. It's beautiful, like him. It reminds me of an enchanting, rare black butterfly that's poisonous if you touch it.

"Just so we're clear," he mutters harshly. "I'm not your brother."

CHAPTER EIGHT

GARRET

THERE IS something about Rose I can't figure out. She occupies my thoughts every waking moment, even when all I want to do is ruin her—break her into pieces so I can create the perfect version of her. But I can't, because she is beautiful the way she is. Lies and all.

What if I ruin the look in her eyes that she reserves only for me? The tremble in her hands when I'm near her. The look that battles between lust and hate.

I sit outside her door, listening, hoping that my name slips from her lips. But it doesn't. It's always "stop," followed by the sadness in her cries—cries that fill my soul.

I'm fucked up. I know I am, and it's no secret. I'm a killer, and I enjoy pain.

I was ordered to kill her—an order given when a Prey knows too much. She's a liability, but I can't.

John still doesn't know the real reason for my visit. All he knows is that the Order sent me to meet her. They know we've talked on campus. There are cameras, and I don't care if they saw me come all over her hands. They've seen worse.

But I couldn't help myself. I want to degrade her, show her how my hate spills from my cock for wanting her the way I do. Even if I can't fuck her because she'll ruin me if I did.

"Where are you taking me?" she asks in a fragile voice pulling me from my thoughts

I wish I could tell that I'm going to kill her and be done with it, but I can't. Not yet.

I had a spot picked out near the abandoned house the consortium uses for its victims. The others don't know the Order wants her dead. Not Valen, the twins, Reid, Azriel, Melody, Veronica, Gia, or Jess. They're not supposed to. All they know is she's on her own until she graduates, but what they don't know is that they signed her death warrant.

"Wherever I want," I say instead.

She looks away, staring at the dark-tinted window. The silence is thick with tension, unlit, waiting for the right spark. I'm not sure what I'm even doing being this close to her.

All I know is that I couldn't leave her there with him. The way he looks at her disgusts me. It's like the sharp end of a knife slicing my skin open.

I pull into the famous diner where all the sons of Kenyan have taken their wives. Except she isn't going to be anyone's wife. Ever.

"You didn't have to offer," she says suddenly. "I couldn't have stayed."

"You like the attention John gives you?" She glances at me with sadness and hate in her eyes every time his name is mentioned, and I don't know why she doesn't leave. Why she accepts the way he treats her for money. Why she told the biggest lie to the only people who could protect her.

And I hate her for it.

"Let's go." I get out, not waiting for her answer. It's probably just another lie, and I don't want another reason to kill her.

Walking up the steps, I turn around, waiting for her to get out of the car. I'm not chivalrous. I surprised myself when I opened her door to begin with. I wait a few seconds while she contemplates getting out of the car. I press the unlock button on the key fob, hoping she gets the hint from the clicking sound. A few guys from Ohio State Walk up in their letterman jackets right when she steps out of the car.

The guys stop whatever they were saying, and one of them mutters, "Damn," staring at the car. But when she straightens her faded sweater, trying to cover the sliver of skin on her small waist because it's a size too small, outlining the generous amount of breasts underneath, I notice it's not my Rolls Spectre they're looking at, as I'm used to, but her.

The feeling of possessiveness when another man looks at her drives me insane when it shouldn't. The way their greedy gaze slides over every curve, thinking of all the ways they could fuck her. The way these assholes are doing now. The way Luke did when he asked her to my party. What I had to do to Luke's face when he said he was going to fuck her. Why I marked her with my cum and warned her not to go.

The one wearing a fucking cowboy hat steps forward and says, "Hi." I recognize him. He's this year's new quarterback for Ohio State from Texas. She smiles awkwardly, and annoyance settles in the pit of my stomach. "Nice car."

What a loser.

"It's not mine," she says truthfully.

"Ahh… boyfriend," he says, fishing for the truth. She

shakes her head. I watch in slow motion as his eyes light up like she gave him the greatest gift in the world. Her voice and an opening to keep talking to her. Stealing her eyes, her voice, and her time when they weren't his. "I'm—"

"In the way," I interrupt him scornfully. He looks up, and so do his stupid friends. I watch his expression turn to shock when he recognizes me. "What's up, Garret?" he says nervously, looking between me and Rose. "Could you move? I'm kind of hungry." I open the door wider, forcefully holding it open, arching my brow at Rose to hurry the fuck up before I stab him in the eyes, break his fucking hands, and cut out his tongue. Rose doesn't argue and moves like it started to rain.

Dorathy smiles when she places the menus on the table, her matchmaking eyes shifting between me and Rose. "I haven't seen you here in a while, handsome," she smiles. "Who's the pretty lady?"

Rose grins awkwardly, not knowing what to say, and I'm pissed at the way the asshole keeps looking this way. If it weren't for Dorathy, I would have walked over there. I grab the menu and scan it like I don't know what I want. "Her name is Rose."

"Hi, Rose," Dorathy says brightly. "I'm Dorathy."

Rose smiles, and my chest tightens at how gorgeous she is when her lips stretch, showing her white teeth. One is slightly shifted, and I want the imprint of her bite on my skin. "It's nice to meet you, Dorathy," she replies gently. Dorathy looks at me with pride in her eyes. "She's gorgeous, Garret."

"She's not my girlfriend," I point out.

"Well, I guess some other guy will be lucky to have her then."

Rose looks down at the menu. We both know that isn't going to happen for very different reasons. I place my order. Dorathy patiently waits for Rose. Rose bites the corner of her lip. It's so innocent. I'm not sure she knows she does it. She looks at Dorothy like she's summoning the courage to speak. "Can I have a glass of water and fries? The small basket, please?"

I frown, scanning the menu and finding the small basket of fries where Dorothy created a value menu. A small basket of fries is $2.95. What the fuck? "She'll have the special, Dorothy," I order. "Burger, large fry, and a strawberry milkshake."

Dorothy smiles, ignoring Rose's panicked expression. "There we go," she says, taking the menus. When Dorothy is out of earshot, something flashes in Rose's eyes. "Why did you do that?"

"Because you're too skinny, and you need to eat."

"Why the fuck do you care?" she says, as if I offended her.

"Hmm… I like this side of you so much better. You should let out whatever the fuck is keeping you from speaking up. I know there's a wildfire inside waiting to be lit."

She rolls her eyes.

"And you're the fucking match, right?"

"Is that what you want, Rose?" I lean close. "You want me to be your match?"

Her pupils go wide. Her brown eyes are so rich, I would pay anything to drown in them.

Her straight hair frames her face, so pretty and delicate. I bet my hands would leave dents a flat iron couldn't straighten.

"Why are you doing this?" she asks, looking around

the red-and-white decorated diner like she's never been to one.

"I don't know what you mean. I was hungry and bored with useless people. Don't read too much into it. I said I would make sure you ate, and unlike you, I keep my promises."

"Like you did to your girlfriend, Cassie," she says sardonically. I smile when I see jealousy the spark of jealousy in her eyes. "I thought we talked about this. I don't have a girlfriend."

"But you told your mother…"

"I said I kept my promises. I never said I didn't lie."

"What promise is that?"

I lean back. "Well, that depends."

"On?" she presses, trying to sound tough.

"What I want," I say truthfully.

"What do you want?" she asks, curiously, but I can tell deep down she's afraid of the answer.

Her eyes tell me what her words can't. She's afraid I want her. That I would break the wall we've built between us. A wall we couldn't break because we weren't sure if we would survive once we crossed it, but I have to kill her.

And then there's the part of me that can't end her without me in it.

CHAPTER NINE

AFTER WE ATE, I was glad the guys from Ohio took the hint. I don't know what came over Garret or why he decided to order me so much food. How did he know I would love a strawberry shake?

I lean my head back and stare at the stars twinkling on the black ceiling of his car. I didn't think cars were equipped with stars on the ceiling. It's dark but alive at the same time—beautiful with minimal light.

"They come with the car," he says, as if he's reading my thoughts.

I look out the window instead, watching my dorm building flash by. "Where are you taking me?"

"I need to stop at my house first," he replies, as if he's just going to sleep over.

"You could drop me off, so you don't have to go back," I reason, trying to hide the panic threatening to rise in my stomach.

I don't want to go to his house, where it smells like him. Where I know what his sheets feel like, only to see them gone. Where I remember him bathing me and shaving me bare, where he told me I was disgusting.

He doesn't respond, and it enrages me further, but I don't push. I'm afraid he'll snap.

He pulls into his driveway, and the garage door automatically opens to reveal a row of cars I've heard people talk about around John, like their precious collectibles. Different makes and models, but all share the same color:

black. There are at least five or six, including the one we're in. He parks in the empty spot and shuts off the car.

He closes the garage, and I watch through the rearview mirror with horror as it descends like a trapdoor.

"Get out," he says, his voice a deep whisper that sends goosebumps erupting across my skin.

I do as he says, taking my bag and following him inside.

A shiver runs down my spine. What would John do to me if he found out? How would I survive his jealous wrath? "How long is this going to take? I have class tomorrow."

He looks over his shoulder, and the intense look in his eyes makes me shudder. "As long as it takes." His words float above me like dust in the late afternoon sun, with nowhere to go.

I walk to the couch in the living room and sit, avoiding the hallway he disappeared into. His house is grand and opulent like John and Mary's, but decorated differently. I can tell things have been removed and replaced. There's a cream and red chair that Mary would have picked out, with giant black letters spray-painted across it that read, CUNT.

Anyone could tell a man lives here. The rest of the furniture is black and gold. It looks Italian—modern, with a mix of traditional pieces like gilded mirrors and frames on the walls. Italian chairs surround a large rug with the same baroque details as the sheets in the room.

The rich black leather couch is modern yet comfortable. I take a deep breath, and a sense of calm washes over me. I can see myself in a house like this, with a man who loves me—sitting right in this exact spot, reading a book and waiting for my husband to come home from work to kiss me. A fairytale I could get lost in.

I wake up with a jolt and a shuddering sob. I look around and remember I'm not in my dorm. The smell of cinnamon teases my nose. The room spins, and I blink rapidly, hoping it will stop. I clutch my stomach, telling myself I'm safe and that I fell asleep, but then I remember that I'm in Garret's house, and he never took me back to my dorm.

He disappeared.

It's dark except for the light from the glowing flames of the electric fireplace. I grip the sheet covering my body and notice it's the same one from that night.

"Do you always cry when you sleep?" My heart threatens to burst out of my chest. I wipe the tears off my cheeks with a clammy hand.

Garret is sitting in a single chair deep in the shadows, watching me.

Studying me.

"What time is it?" I ask, my throat raw.

"A little after one a.m."

The last thing I want to tell him is about my nightmares. I pull the sheet away. "It's really late. I should be heading back."

"I didn't want to wake you," he says, as if he cares.

"So you watched me sleep?"

He gets up, and I try not to cower when he walks toward me. "Come," he says, then turns around, heading down the same hallway he disappeared from, illuminated by long black modern sconces on the wall.

I grab my bag and sheet, dragging them along with me until he stops in front of the door. There are so many down the long hallway; I don't remember which one I was in the last time I was here. All I could think about was leaving when the Uber arrived.

When he opens it, familiarity blankets me. The king-sized bed that felt like a cloud sits in the center of the room, like a bottomless pool of comfort.

I walk in and freeze. Something black moves toward me, and I step back in fear when the dog with the spiked collar growls.

I step back further.

Then a few steps more until my back hits something warm, hard, and solid.

"Shhh…" His breath fans my hair, causing goosebumps to spread along the side of my neck. "Don't show him fear. Fear is what feeds the attack. Fear is what breaks you inside."

"That's because he isn't about to shred you into pieces."

"It's his protective instinct."

"That's why you need to take me home," I argue.

The massive Doberman seizes the moment to run up to me and sniff the sheets, then my legs. I turn my head to the side, a scream threatening to rise from my throat. The dog looks up, the dark orbs of his eyes resting on me as he sits on his back legs, analyzing whether I'm a threat.

Garret snaps his fingers. "Ace, stay," he commands. The dog walks back to the foot of the bed and lies on the floor. "He knows your scent," Garret rasps, inhaling the aroma of my skin. Heat spreads over my body to the juncture between my thighs. I can feel the stubble from his cheek against my temple, his breath fanning my ear. "You have nothing to be afraid of. Watch."

The dog observes

us, his eyes following Garret's hand as it slides around

my throat. "Ace is a good judge of character. He keeps coming back to this room looking for you."

I don't know how to interpret that statement or how I should feel about it.

The dog growls when Garret's hand tightens around my neck, stealing my breath. I should shove him away, but I'm terrified of what the dog might do. Will he attack? Will he shred me to pieces before Garret can stop him?

"He's not growling at you, Rose. He's growling at me for touching you." The dog's ears point to the ceiling, and his snout is wet. Garret is right; he doesn't look happy.

"How is that possible?"

"Ace is moody and overprotective when he sees something he likes—something worth protecting." The dog whines and lowers his head, unsure of what to do. "See, even my dog wants you, Rose." His lips skim my neck, causing my nipples to harden. My knees threaten to buckle. "You're safe here."

He releases me, and it feels like stepping into the dark, cold night when he moves away.

"If you want to take a shower, it's through the door to your left," he says, pausing at the threshold. "There's a robe and a towel in the warmer. I'm sure you know how the shower works."

I turn around, but he's already gone.

"Read this part here," Azriel says, pointing to the paragraph.

I'm struggling in my Literature class. I thought math would be a problem, but once the professor told us we had to write an analysis on a selection of written works, I didn't know what to do. I had no choice; I had to sign up with Azriel for more tutoring.

I begin, but I struggle by the fourth word. I stop and glance at Azriel. My heart sinks when I see the grimace on his face.

"It's bad," I say with a frustrated sigh.

"Has it always been like this?" Azriel asks softly, a pitying look in his gaze.

"I struggle a bit," I confess, placing a strand of hair behind my ear.

He stares at my assignment, and I know he must be thinking there is no way I'll pass. There are times I want to give up and let them fail me, but my pride gets in the way. I know that if I had the right schooling, the right opportunity, I would succeed. I get the assignment, but I have to read to understand it. It's like trying to fix a car with no tools.

He scratches his brow. "Do you have friends in your class that you can study with? Someone in the dorm who can help? Read it to you?"

I hadn't thought about making friends in my classes for the purpose of studying. I can't think of anything, knowing I'm on my own in a place like this, considering what I do. Who do I trust?

You trust Garret enough to stay in his house.

He took me to school instead of ordering an Uber this morning. He dropped me off in front of my dorm without a word and then drove off.He also made sure I had a bowl of fruit on a tray in my room in the morning, as well as new clothes in my size.

I don't know what to think or why he did it, but I'm grateful.

"I didn't think I could make a friend." He looks up.

"You know, after everything." I scan the library as if someone is out to get me at any second.

"It doesn't work like that," he says, lowering his voice.

I lean forward. "How does it work exactly?"

Any help I can get will be welcome at this point. Staying at Garret's house has clouded my judgment. John hasn't texted me. It's as if Garret has the power to keep him away, and I don't know what to make of it.

"Keep to yourself and don't fall into a trap."

"What do you mean?" I ask curiously. I don't have a guy in the Order who is in love with me and will keep me safe.

The current one ruling the school hates my existence. Garret doesn't want me; he wants to destroy me.

"You say no at all costs, Rose. Do you hear me?" I nod. "If any asshole corners you, you say no. And you don't go anywhere where you might find yourselfalone with them, especially Garret."

"What about me?"

My stomach flips.

Garret takes the seat next to Azriel, looking at him as if he wants to slit his throat and play with his vocal cords.

Azriel looks at him unfazed and then at me. "I was warning Rose to be careful on campus."

"I heard my name," Garret points out. Then he glances at the designer sweater he left on the dresser this morning, as if he's peeling it off my chest. "Nice sweater." He gives me a wink.

My cheeks flush. Azriel looks at me and then back at Garret. "What are you doing, Garret?" Azriel says in a hard tone, like he's scolding a child.

"I came to say hi." He glances at my assignment in front of Azriel. "You need help?"

"No."

Ignoring me, Garret picks up the paper with the list of works to choose from for an analysis. He scans the list and places it on the table, turning it around to point. "Edgar Allan Poe's *Annabel Lee.*"

Azriel looks at me. We both know it would be difficult for me to read and analyze.

"She's going to need a lot of help with that one," Azriel begins.

"I'll help her," Garret says, snatching the paper. "You can help her with the math and stuff. I'll help her with this."

I'm about to protest, but Garret gets up and walks out as if his word is final and I've agreed to let him help me.

"Fuck," Azriel says, rubbing his eyes.

I watch Garret through the glass window, wanting to stab him when he smiles at a group of girls.

"Why?"

"Because he's fucking crazy," Azriel mutters, as if that's supposed to make me feel better.

"What do I do now?"

"Nothing," he says. "There's nothing you can do, Rose. The guys messed with him when he was younger. He got into some trouble and was always the crazy kid left alone in his big house, getting whatever he wanted. Then his father died two years ago, and he spiraled. He was put on medication. When his mother remarried after being left with nothing, he went dark. It was as if the lights were on, but no one was home. No one—and I mean no one—could change his mind once he set it on something. He smiles, laughs, plays along. But some of us know it's all a lie. Garret doesn't give a shit. He does whatever he wants."

"What makes him so different from your brother or… the others?"

He exhales forcefully through his nose. "Simple. Garret doesn't answer to anyone. He doesn't have a father to respect because he's dead. His mother even less, because all she cares about is her Bentley and how much is in her bank account. He basically grew up fending for himself in his father's mansion, and it's no different now that he's dead. The only people he answers to are the Order. He has everything at his disposal." He snorts. "Garret has so much money that there's no way he can spend it all in three lifetimes. What does a man with power and an unlimited bank account do?"

The most I've had was twenty dollars to last me three days before I had to spend it. "I wouldn't know."

"Whatever the hell he wants. The Nox family has power and connections, and he's the only Nox left. That is what makes Garret dangerous, Rose. He can do anything because his father made sure of it."

CHAPTER TEN

THE ROOM FILLS with students when the professor walks in. I make my way toward the back, where a girl with strawberry blond hair sits.

She takes out a notebook from her bag.

Being around the others last year, I can tell she's prey. Her clothes are not designer, and the deer-in-the-head-lights look she gives the others gives it away. The privileged here are cocky and stand out. They know everyone, and if you stay in the dorms, you'll recognize certain faces. I've seen her a couple of times but never thought to talk to her until now.

I'm sure Azriel is taking a huge risk in helping me. I still don't know why, but the least I can do is help myself. This is something I can control. That gives me hope. Garret knowing I could barely read and write is too much of a risk. He isn't going to be there when John finds out and gets ahold of me. It also shows weakness—a vulnerability that isn't wise to share with someone like him.

The intense way Azriel looked at me when he spoke about Garret set off an alarm bell in the back of my head—a warning I recognize when something bad is brewing. Garret showing up wasn't a mere coincidence. He's watching me like a predator does when he's already caught his prey and is waiting for the right time to kill it, and Azriel, he's doing his best to try to warn me.

"Is this seat taken?" I ask. She looks up with wide eyes and then grins.

"No, go ahead." A sense of relief washes over me.

"Great." I'm awkward around others, and I hope I can pull this off and she doesn't find me weird.

I take out my notebook and open it to the page where I wrote Edgar Allan Poe's name.

"Oh, are you working on that one?" she asks.

I nod. "Yeah," I say, glad for the opening I need.

"That's a tough one, I think. I'm doing this one." She points at the sheet Garret took the other day—the one I need to get back. I can't read the one she's pointing at because she pulls the paper away before I can make out the words. Fuck. This is not going the way I planned. "Hey, if you want, we could go over it together."

I raise my brows hopefully. "Alright."

"We could critique each other's work. Maybe hang out."

It's like a huge weight has lifted off my chest. She gives me her number and tells me her name is Amy. She asks where I hang out and what my dorm number is. I tell her I don't have a specific place. I agree to her invite to a small party off campus.

I forget about John and Garret. I forget about my past and my nightmares.

For the first time, it feels like I can breathe. I don't have to lie to this girl. I don't have to pretend. I listen to every single word the professor says, trying to take notes the best I can—in a way I can understand. He drones on about what is required for the assignment and, of course, a reminder of when it's due—two weeks from today.

I'm about to walk to my dorm room after my last class when my phone goes off.

Unknown: Meet me after class. Pool.

I don't have to guess who it's from, and I won't bother

to ask how he got my number. I also don't want to piss him off, so I walk toward the indoor pool on campus. I've never seen the guys at swim practice—not with Melody or the others. We always met up in the quad or at the bar across the street.

I don't know what to expect, but when I pull the door open and the smell of chlorine hits me in the face, it isn't this. The bleachers are filled with people—mostly girls fangirling over the guys wearing swim trunks. I can't blame them. Their bodies are perfection.

There isn't an ounce of body fat on them, but then I notice this is not a practice but a swim meet. On the other side of the pool, there are more guys half-naked—abs and muscles made to snatch a girl's attention. Someone whistles, snagging my attention, and I realize it's the coach from the Kenyan swim team getting the team together. I spot Garret, and my heart almost stops. He's gorgeous. My mouth goes dry. He stands above most of the guys, but his tattoos ripple along with his muscles when he moves. I've only seen him with his clothes on, and I knew he was ripped, but the man is dangerous in every way. It's hard not to stare. I walk up the bleachers on the home team side and sit in the empty row on top to get a clear view of the pool.

"Let's go, Nox!" a girl screams. Garret turns around and grins. My heart sinks when I see it's Cassie. She blows him a kiss, and I get the sudden urge to grab her by the hair and drown her. I don't know why he asked me to come. He obviously has plenty of fans. I'm about to get up, but then someone waves in my direction while standing next to Garret. I notice it's Luke. I look behind me and then back. He waves again, catching Garret's attention. I notice he has a large cut on his lip and wonder how he got it, but then I feel Garret's gaze on my skin. He shakes his head slowly in warning. I sit, letting him think I'm staying. I don't like the attention I'm getting from everyone.

Cassie looks over her shoulder; when she spots me, she sneers, "Don't think about it, bitch. I saw you watching us like some kind of creep." People turn and stare at me like I'm a stalker. I could pretend that her words don't sting, that the laughter from her friends doesn't crawl under my skin. The mocking glances from the others as they whisper only heighten my discomfort. I keep my head down, knowing there is no point in telling Cassie to go fuck herself. There are more of them and one of me. There is no one who would help me or come to my defense. Like always, I have no one. Tears burn behind my eyes, but I make sure to look away. "Is she going to cry?" Cassie says loud enough for everyone to hear. I get up to leave before the last bit of my pride snaps, and I do something I will later regret. I shouldn't have come here. Fuck her. And fuck them. These entitled pricks aren't worth it. I walk out, the cold air smacking me in the face. I take a deep breath to steady the hammering of my heart. The weight that was lifted earlier slams back on my chest, trapping me inside. I head for my dorm and decide I will stay inside until school tomorrow morning. I can get something to eat from the vending machine. I'm down the hall, about to turn left to get to my door when my name is called.

"Rose?" I turn around. "Amy?" She smiles. "Hey, I was about to knock on your door. Want to grab a drink or a bite to eat across the street?" I smile like she's my savior. "Yeah, I would like that a lot."

· · ·

Babylon is not as packed as the few times I was invited by Melody, most likely because of the swim meet on campus. I'm sure it's only a matter of time before students start pouring in to head to the bar and the pool tables. "Do you know what you're going to wear to the party?" Amy asks after we are shown to a booth. I haven't thought of the party or what I'll wear. The truth is, I have nothing to wear. "I'm not sure." I stare at the small menu on the table, mentally calculating how much I have on my card. The waitress with six piercings on her face and orange hair stops by. Amy orders a beer, and I opt for water. "Oh, no," Amy says with a grin. "Make that two beers."

Before I can protest, the waitress scurries off. "I don't drink."

Amy leans forward. "Please tell me you've had a beer."

I haven't, but I don't want to sound like a prude, so I let it slide. The most I've had is Scotch—a drink I hate as much as the person who gave it to me laced with drugs. It was either needles or Scotch. Both I detest with every fiber of my being. "Not really. I'm not twenty-one."

"I am. I started school late, and my birthday was last month. Besides, she doesn't look the type to ask or give a shit either way."

I'm sure they are told not to when it comes to Prey. There is a different set of rules when it comes to anything involving Kenyan, Babylon included. The waitress comes back with our beer and my water. I take a sip of the amber liquid and hold back a wince from the bitter taste but play it off before she notices. "Who's the guy I saw you with at the library?"

My stomach drops. My thoughts fly to the afternoon on the shelves with Garret. "I'm not sure…"

"Not the swim team captain—the other one."

A sense of relief washes over me like a gust of wind. "Azriel."

Her eyes light up with interest. "So that's his name. I didn't think he went to Kenyan."

"He does, but he's a hybrid student. Mostly online. He tutors."

"He is so cute."

I should tell her to stay away, warn her, but who am I to tell her anything? It would also mean I would have to explain why. Then she would get scared and tell me to fuck off. Two things I can't risk. Azriel is nice, and he isn't evil like the others. He hasn't given me any reason to worry, but that doesn't mean he isn't. He's Valen's brother, after all. I'm sure he's part of something. They all are. "He is nice to look at," I tell her truthfully, and then a sense of protectiveness settles in my gut. I don't know where it came from, but I see Azriel like a brother, the same way he sees Melody like a sister. I shouldn't feel this way after the way things went, but Azriel has been the only one to help me, to warn me. He's shown me that he cares, even if it's stemmed from pity. "I guess I'll have to sign up for tutoring then."

"Be careful; he's a heartbreaker." I don't think I've ever seen Azriel look at another girl, but it's the only thing I can come up with. "You know, I thought he was your boyfriend at first, but then the other guy showed up... Garret is his name, right?"

"I don't have a boyfriend. He was there for Azriel." I hate lying. It's like a disease that acts up when you least expect it, but I don't want to talk about Garret. I came along to make a friend and forget about him. "So, about the party. What are you planning on wearing? I heard it's fun and it's where both Kenyan and Ohio students go to hang out without killing each other."

I've heard of it but have never gone, most likely because my weekends were occupied or I was unconscious. "I've never been invited."

"I haven't gone either. I transferred from another school."

I'm curious to know where she came from. I didn't see her in any of my classes or on campus last year. "What school?"

Her eyes dim, and I can tell there is a story she isn't ready to tell, so I keep it light. I guess we all have stories we are afraid to tell and sometimes ones we can't. "Delaware."

"I've never been."

"Boring. You're not missing anything special." Definitely a story back there. "I applied for a transfer, and this place offered a scholarship based on my GPA. I couldn't say no."

I don't want to rain on her parade and reveal the real reason. It would scare her off, and they wouldn't let her go either way. These people are evil. Once you accept, it's like you've pledged your life in blood, and you didn't even know it. They make sure she will never graduate anywhere else—probably blacklist her wherever she goes. That's why I keep my mouth shut and make it my mission to look out for her. One good deed to erase the lies I've had to spill. She talks about the things she likes, her favorites. I tell her I have none because I don't. There wasn't much to compare anything to with my limited experience, and everything I did try was part of an act I was forced to endure. If it was food, a song, a drink, a smell, or a feeling,

I ended up hating it because it reminded me of the time I had to try it.

Music starts to play, and then voices get louder. Within the hour, the place is crawling with students. My guess is the meet is over, and judging by the happy faces, Kenyan dominated. "Oh my God," Amy says with excitement, bopping her head to the intro. "I love this song. It's 'Everything I Do Is for You' by Amira Elfeky." She glances at the jukebox to see who selected it, and my heart feels like it's going to stop. Garret is standing like a skyscraper. His tall, muscular back underneath a tight long-sleeved shirt molds to his frame. The band of his sweatpants sits on his hips. I can tell he's fresh from a shower. The black strands of his hair on the back of his head are dark like ink from a black marker.

"Is that..." Amy trails off when he turns around, pushing the long strands of his straight hair off his face like a model in a commercial. His face is smooth. His chiseled jaw does things to my insides—the memory of his lips on my skin when he spoke, his breath causing heat to spread to my thighs. It all evaporates when Cassie walks up, standing on her toes and causing her skirt to lift almost above the cheeks of her ass. She is everything I'm not: beautiful with a nice body that guys drool over. He can keep lying all he wants—he's into her. You wouldn't have caught her sucking him off if he wasn't. I tear my gaze away. "Yeah, it was him. Garret."

"He's looking this way," she says, but I don't care. I'm focused on drinking my beer for moral support. I could care less if he told me to meet him after his swim meet and

I left. I'm done being humiliated. "What's going on between you two? The girl with him is glaring this way."

"There is nothing going on. I was friends with him, and now I'm not. They graduated, so… it doesn't matter anymore."

"I don't think he feels the same, judging by the way he's staring. It looks like he wants to kidnap you."

She wouldn't be wrong, but not in the way she thinks. He isn't into me. He's playing games, like they all do to prey, and I'm on the menu. "I don't think his girlfriend, or whatever she is, will be happy about it. She already showed me her claws after I caught her sucking him off in the library." I take a large sip of my beer and place it on the table, letting the heat from the alcohol calm my anxiety. "If you hear about it in the morning, that's what happened. I don't think she was so happy about it."

"Is it because he's ignoring her and staring right at you?"

I sneak a glance. I can't help it. Sure enough, he's leaning on the jukebox like he owns it and staring at me with his black eyes. The heat from his gaze feels like it's threatening to melt my skin.

He heads this way after ignoring Cassie's attempt to grab his attention and storms off. Shit. I stare straight ahead at Amy. I can see apprehension in her expression when he walks up and slides into the booth next to me. "Why did you leave?" he asks, his mouth inches from my cheek. I can feel his eyes rolling over my skin. I turn and stare him down. "Why don't you ask your girlfriend?"

He smiles, but it's not friendly. "She's not my girlfriend."

I arch my brow. "Could have fooled me."

"Yeah, now everyone thinks Rose likes to watch you get it on in the library," Amy chimes in my defense. "Looks serious to me."

Garret shifts in his seat and faces Amy with an unreadable expression. "And you are?"

"Amy," I reply. "She's in my Lit class. We're catching up. We have to study for our current reading assignment."

"Is that right?" he drawls, still looking at Amy. She shifts in her seat under his scrutiny and grabs her beer, chugging the rest in one go. "What do you want, Garret? Don't you have someone waiting for you to nail them to a cross?"

He chuckles darkly. "What a great idea, my little Darkthorn."

"I'm not your anything," I sneer, my tone curling like smoke. I'm done playing this game with him. I won't let him ruin my every waking moment. I have enough with John and his shit. I don't need to add Garret to my mountain of fears. "Hurry up with your little friend," he says dismissively. "You have class tomorrow." He gets up, grabs my half-empty glass of beer, and walks off in the direction of the bar.

"What was that about?" Amy asks after a few seconds.

"I don't know."

Garret heads to the pool table area where Cassie and

her friends are hanging out, drinking shots. He says something to her, and judging by the look on her face from where I'm sitting, she isn't thrilled. She glares in my direction when he walks away and heads back over. "I think I'll see you tomorrow," I say as I get up.

"Sure."

I stop the waitress when she passes by. "Can I have the bill, please?"

"Oh, your boyfriend took care of it," she announces with a smile and a wink before she walks off with her tray. My eyes dart to Amy. "Don't stay up too late," she beams, as if I'm going to hook up with a celebrity. If she only knew.

CHAPTER ELEVEN

GARRET

"SHE DOESN'T HAVE the right blood, Garret. You know the rules."

"Neither did Veronica," I reply.

Alaric's gaze hardens. I struck a nerve. He hates when another man speaks his beloved wife's name. But I saved her—more than once. Not in the way he would like. But in a way, she saved me.

It's true. She was supposed to be in the dorms, but the sadistic bastard her mother married wouldn't allow it.

"True," Caruthers agrees. He's the oldest one in the room so he gets the final ruling when it comes to Prey.

But I can see the wheels turning in the old man's head. He's playing right into my game. And he doesn't even know it.

"And what do you propose?"

I don't hesitate. "She stays with me."

"Absolutely not!" John roars.

I smirk. It's not up to him. No one but Caruthers and the others—the real players in this game—know why I have to be involved.

Valen and Reid watch me with interest. They haven't decided how they want this to end. But I have.

Rose is mine. I want to peel her apart, layer by layer. She only gives me glimpses. But she's pulling away. I can see it in her eyes— She's giving up on me. A girl like her doesn't stay interested for long. She's taught herself not to trust. It's what people do when lying is their only choice.

"It's not up to you, John," Caruthers says. "It's up to me. You're lucky we don't kill you for the deception."

John's face darkens. "She gets nothing." He looks at me triumphantly.

I want to laugh in his face. "You think I'm conspiring, John?" I grin. "I have more money than your entire pathetic existence—your forefathers included—sitting in my bank account. I wouldn't burn through that amount if I died four times and came back. So please, don't insult yourself. I can smell your shit from here." I glance at Caruthers. "She stays with me. Until I see fit."

Caruthers exhales, impatient. "Fine." His voice cuts through the tension like a blade. "Enough talk about a girl with no future in our organization."

John's fury ignites. "You won't get away with this, Nox." He glares, seething. "I own her. She's mine."

I pick up my plague mask from the pew. "Please, try and stop me." My tone is dry, amused. But inside— I want to smash his face in.

I want to gut him open and play jump rope with his intestines.

———

Alaric meets me outside after the others leave. "What the fuck, Nox? You want your bloodline to die?"

I shrug. "I didn't mean to mention her. But it was the only way."

He adjusts his tailored suit jacket, the red Louis Vuitton

tie unmistakably Veronica's choice. He never would have picked that out himself. Let alone worn a fucking tie. "A way to get your little toy out of the playpen?"

I scoff. "You would've done the same." I pause. "I need a favor."

He snorts. "What? You want my fucking balls? My cock? You want that too?" "I need Veronica to stop by the house."

He laughs. It's murderous. "Like fucking hell. You had a better chance with my dick."

"It's not for me. It's for her."

He rolls his shoulders. "Ask any other asshole's wife you've fucked in the past. Why does it have to be mine?"

I exhale. "Jess is eight months pregnant. Melody wouldn't understand. And the twins don't let Gia out of their sight." I meet his gaze. "Veronica's the only one I trust."

He studies me. "Why her?"

I give him the real answer. "She's the only one who understands me."

Alaric walks to the cemetery entrance. The clouds shift, revealing the full moon. He sighs. "I should have hit you harder that day." His voice is flat. "I thought the pills we slipped you would teach you a lesson."

I shake my head. "That wasn't funny." He smirks. "I thought I had small dick syndrome for a year until the doctor told me about the side effects."

He grins, unrepentant. "You should have kept it in your pants before you fucked with Jess. It was Reid's idea."

Fucking assholes.

I shake my head. "Tell him he owes me."

"I think knowing you've tasted our wife's pussy is punishment enough."

I glare. "I said I was sorry."

Alaric exhales.

"What is it with you and this girl?"

I don't respond.

He continues.

"Melody wants to reach out to her. You said no. Repeatedly. And now this."

I hesitate. "I don't know yet. But I need you to find out where John adopted her from." He goes still. "There are no records. Something doesn't add up."

Alaric leans against the stone pillar. The moonlight catches in his dark eyes.

He finally nods. "Well, for one thing—John's a liar." He straightens. "It's obvious he's possessive of her."

"She has nightmares." I exhale. "The way she cries. The way she pleads."

Alaric's jaw tics. "Like Veronica did?"

I stare at my father's grave. "Yeah."

The tombstone doesn't say beloved father. Or beloved husband. Because he was neither.

He became a monster the day my mother terminated every child he put inside her—except me. I thought he hated me for being the only one she chose to keep. But it wasn't hatred. It was pity. He used me against her.

He was a liar, a killer, a deceiver. But he loved his legacy. And that meant, in his twisted way—he loved me.

I was his sole heir to the Nox estate, the fortune, the company—mine.

No stipulations. No forced marriage. No need for heirs.

I could have walked away. But then Rose showed up. She witnessed corruption. She saw death. And didn't run.

She took it and it means she's seen it before. It means she's suffered.

The Order sends students to Kenyan because they have some type of mental condition. Me included. But what if the Order made a mistake? What if Rose is the sanest one of us all?

CHAPTER TWELVE

THERE IS a knock on my door. I place the bag of potato chips on the old nightstand next to the soda. I mark the page of the passage from *Edgar Allan Poe* and get up.

There is no peephole. Someone messed up the hole, and I can't see who it is.

I've told security multiple times, and they said someone from maintenance should have come up to fix it, but no one has arrived. I gave up after the third request.

"Who is it?" I call out.

Nothing. It's not Amy because she said she would call me tomorrow to go shopping. I didn't want to tell her I didn't have money to buy anything, but I didn't want to miss out on some girl time. She wouldn't just stand there and say nothing. She comes in like a ball of energy the few times we've hung out.

They knock again.

"Who is it?" I repeat.

Nothing.

I kick the door. "I guess you can keep knocking because I'm not going to open the door until you tell me who you are."

Knock. Knock.

I sigh in frustration. "Who's there?"

A paper slides under my door. Is this some kind of joke?

I pick up the sheet of note paper. I DON'T KNOCK.

"What?"

The lights flicker off, and my blood turns cold.

"I'm already inside." Garret's breath floats over my skin. He's right behind me.

Sweat trickles from the nape of my neck down my spine. I whirl around, but I can't see him. It's dark, but I can smell him.

"What are you doing?"

"I came to tutor you."

Like hell he is. I walk toward the light switch, but he grabs me and tosses me onto the small bed. "Get off me," I yell. His weight is crushing me on the mattress, but it's not enough to stop me from breathing.

"This will only take a second." He pulls the string on the lamp on the nightstand. I swear he must have night vision because I wouldn't have known where to pull.

Warm light spreads around the room like the glowing sun. The only darkness comes from the dark eyes pinning me to the mattress. His gaze trails over the T-shirt I use to sleep in, stopping at the two points of my nipples.

"It's cold," I reply.

He looks up, and his pitch-dark eyes are like two moons during the phase of an eclipse because of the light. "Then I should warm you up," he breathes. His mouth is on my neck, his hot breath warming my skin. I try to squeeze my legs together, but all I do is straddle his hips, pushing him into me. His mouth trails over my left breast, hovering over my nipple beneath the thin T-shirt. "Is this how you study?" His eyes pause on my hard nipple. "Dressed like this?"

I can smell the scent of his shampoo from his hair tickling my chin. His cock is pressed against my panties through his black jeans, causing my pussy to ache.

"Garret," I croak, not knowing what to say or how to move.

How did he get in here without using the door? It means he could get in here whenever he wants.

"Yes, my little Darkthorn?"

I swallow thickly, wondering why he calls me that. "Why do you call me Darkthorn?"

He arches his back and removes his shirt in one go.

My eyes are lost in a world of black ink. It's everywhere except on his gorgeous face—angels, skulls, demons, and flowers. It's almost too much until I stop on his heart: the petals of black roses with large thorns piercing a heart. The heart is bleeding black ink.

He grabs my hand and places it over his heated skin, right where the thorn pierces the heart. Right where his heart beats. "I have never been in love," he says, his hand warm and firm over mine. "I thought I had, but it wasn't love. Because the greatest love hurts. It's kind of like the feeling when you lose a parent. I imagine when it finds me, it will hurt. It will come from something beautiful—a rose with hidden thorns. Painful if touched, yet impossible to resist. I will bleed, and it will consume my soul." He pauses, and his expression darkens. "You remind me of a Darkthorn."

"It's best if you don't touch me then."

He pushes away from me, taking his scent and warmth with him, leaving me feeling empty.

I pull the hem of my t-shirt down to cover my thighs and sit up. He moves to the small closet. "What are you doing?"

He slides the brown door open. "Getting your things."

"For?"

He turns around, glancing around the room before looking back at the closet. "Where's the rest? A suitcase?"

I grab my black backpack from in front of the night-stand and place it on the bed. "This is it. Now tell me why you need to get my things."

He stares at the black backpack, then at me, as if he thinks I'm joking. I wish I weren't. There isn't much I was given, but why should he care?

He hesitates, then grabs the bag and stuffs the few items I have hanging on the mismatched hangers the previous student left. Once he's done, he looks around the room as if he's about to be evicted, grabbing papers and notebooks from the small desk.

"Toiletries?" I point to the small shower caddy from the dollar store. He picks it up like he's checking for rotten potatoes and drops it on the desk with a thud. He scans the room one more time. When he's satisfied he didn't miss anything, he says, "Let's go."

"Where?"

"To my house." A fluttering sensation fills my lower belly. "You're not staying in the dorm anymore."

"Who said that?"

"The Order."

I almost choke on my spit and stammer, "T-the Order?"

"Yeah, the people who run things around here, and that includes me. You're stay with me."

"Until when?" I ask. "What if you throw me out, and I don't have a dorm to go back to? How about John?"

He pushes his hair out of his eyes in frustration. "Relax with the word vomit. It's getting late. We still have to study, and you need a shower."

"Are you saying I smell?"

He snorts and points at the shower caddy he discarded

like a sack of potatoes. "No, but you can't call that soap. It should be illegal in all fifty states."

"Tell that to John and the twenty bucks he gives me a week. What am I supposed to do?"

He glances at the half-eaten bag of chips, and a look of disgust crosses his features.

Yeah, not everyone is born with a silver spoon in their mouth.

———

I'm back in his car, heading for his mansion four blocks away. It takes about six minutes to reach his house and another three to finally park in his garage. A thought crosses my mind after he puts the car in park and shuts the garage door.

"Where will I go when you throw one of your lavish parties?"

He opens the door. "I haven't thought that far yet."

Flashes of him with girls like Cassie in the king-sized bed make me want to throw up. I slam the car door shut harder than necessary.

"What's wrong, my little Darkthorn? Your thoughts getting ahead of you?"

It's like he knows what I'm thinking. Am I that transparent? Does he see the way I look at him, the way he unravels me with his dark gaze?

"I don't have any thoughts when it comes to you," I snap and walk inside as if this is my house.

I head down the hallway, remembering the bedroom he always takes me to, but then I recall the flash of black and the pointy ears. I pause at the threshold and scan the room.

Awareness skates down my spine. "You like this room, don't you?"

"It's the room you always leave me in."

I haven't had the chance to explore the huge house, something I might do when he isn't around.

He chuckles, and I feel it all the way to my toes. "Whose room do you think it belongs to?"

My heart races as I stare at the bed that belongs to him. It's why the sheets smell so good—they're slept in by him. The decor and the painting all make sense, but why would he bring me to his room and let me sleep in his sheets? Sheets he didn't burn because they are still here.

"You didn't burn the sheets."

"I planned on bringing you back. I had them washed instead."

I didn't burn the clothes he gave me either. I kept them like precious souvenirs because I knew I could never afford something so luxurious, but deep down, the real reason was that they were his. No one had to know, but I'm sure he noticed when he grabbed my things.

"Why? The last time, you seemed hell-bent on getting rid of me. Won't I contaminate them?"

He moves past me, pulls clothes in my size from a drawer, and places them on the made bed. "I'll take my chances."

It's another designer hoodie and a pair of black leggings. This is the sixth outfit he has chosen from the closet. A tiny flutter rises in my stomach knowing he picked them out and placed them in a drawer in his room.

"Where are you going to sleep?"

He steps closer, his scent a breeze that permeates the air between us. "In the bedroom next door."

"Why not put me in that room? Why this one?"

Why does he want me in his room, on his bed? The thought of sleeping in his sheets feels personal. I'm not sure what to make of it.

"Because no one comes in this one except Ace. Not the housekeeper, not a friend if they show up, not when I have a party, or a girl I want to fuck."

At least I'm not sleeping in cum-infested sheets. I should be grateful, considering it's him. Who knows how many women he's been with?

"At least I won't catch anything."

He smiles, and I think my heart skipped a beat or slowed down. "Funny, that is the part you're most worried about—me fucking someone else."

"No more than you. I distinctly remember you pointing out my pussy. I also want to note that you made sure you shaved it."

"Correction, I bathed you. Thoroughly."

"I was unconscious. You're lucky I didn't claw your eyes out."

He leans close, his breath skimming my ear. "We both know you would have let me."

I push him away, and he laughs. The motherfucker laughs.

My blood boils, threatening to explode inside my veins. "Am I a joke to you?"

He stops laughing. His sexy mouth hardens, and his darker side makes an appearance. I wonder how many people have seen this side of him. It's terrifying. His eyes grow hard, like an animal in the dark, ready to pounce.

I step back, cursing myself for letting my mouth get the best of me. An uneasy feeling replaces the flutters in my stomach.

"You being here is not a joke, Rose. You should be nice

to me. After all, I'm keeping the monster that keeps you awake at night inside his cage. I'm also generous enough to give you better accommodations."

He means John, but I don't buy it. My internal alarm is going off. There is something he isn't telling me, and I have a nagging feeling in the back of my mind. I've been taken from one trapped door to another. My fate is sealed.

Garret is a psychopath. He is popular but hides his true nature from others. He is cold. The way he dismissed Cassie after he'd been intimate with her, not caring if he hurt her feelings, speaks volumes. His impulsivity in bringing me here that first night shows he lies and is manipulative. Flashy cars and the over-the-top designer items he buys, are just a way to inflate his ego.

It's why he's at Kenyan.

"Your mind is turning," he says with a smile, but his eyes are distant. "I can practically hear the wheels turning in that pretty head of yours."

"You're going to kill me."

He angles his head to the side. "Is that what you think?"

Dread pools in the back of my eyes, forming tears that threaten to fall. There is a huge ball lodged in my throat, robbing me of speech. I nod.

He claps. "Congratulations. Now you know the reason you're here." He moves to leave. "Don't forget to wash up. I'll order you something to eat."

"I'm not hungry," I blurt, thankful I found my voice.

He pulls open the door wider, allowing Ace to saunter in, his nails clacking on the marble floors. "I don't think you have a choice." He snaps his fingers. Ace lays on the floor at the foot of the bed. "Promises, remember?"

"Fuck you." I'm past caring. If he was sent to kill me,

fine. It's what I've been wishing for anyway. At least he has the balls to do it. I'm sure he wouldn't lose sleep over it.

I still can't believe I agreed stay here with him. Maybe it's self-preservation knowing that John wouldn't show up. There is something freeing knowing that I'm safe from him while I'm here. John is afraid of Garret. I don't know why but maybe I do if Melody's actions that day with Melissa is a hint of the depravity Garret is capable of. Images from the day Melody stabbed Melissa to death flash like a horror movie thinking of all the ways I'll be his victim.

I'm crying for not being strong enough. I don't care if he sees. Psychopaths don't feel. I could cry and sob my heart out, and he wouldn't flinch—just like he isn't now.

"I think we've established how I feel about your cunt."

How could I forget?

I smile. He must think I'm unstable—crying and smiling at the same time—but I won't go down without a fight. Even with my limited ability to read people, I've managed to figure out the basics about those who are mentally disturbed. I wanted to understand what I was dealing with when it came to John and the others; Garret is the classic type of psycho.

"What's so funny?" he asks.

He's trying to hide his confusion, but he's failing. I'm supposed to be crying and trembling, not smiling and laughing when he's about to leave the room. "This whole time, I've been around the one person who would kill me and end all my problems."

"What the fuck are you saying?"

"You asked me the other day if there was something I wanted more than anything. Death."

He flinches, not expecting my revelation. He thought I wanted white picket fences and a savior.

"Death is the one thing I want more than anything, Garret. You killing me is my greatest wish. I'm hoping you can bury me in Kenyan's cemetery right next to the church that decides my fate. I have a spot picked out."

He storms out, slamming the door behind him. The force rattles the painting representing envy on the wall. I walk up to it and trace my finger over the bone on the woman's hand.

CHAPTER THIRTEEN

GARRET

SHE WANTS TO DIE, and she's okay with me being the one to do it. But why? It's not what I expected her to say. Who the hell is okay with dying? She didn't cry out or scream like I thought she would, and none of it makes sense. Why would she go through all the trouble with John if she wanted to die? She could've just jumped off a roof or something.

You would stop her. Someone would. There are cameras everywhere.

I close my eyes, pushing the thought away.

My phone vibrates in my front jeans pocket.

I fish it out.

Alaric: Make sure you go to class. I have the info you asked for. My assistant will be in shortly to explain. I trust it will be an educational experience.

Garret: I thought you graduated like a million years ago.

Alaric: Stop hating because I'm smarter than you, and don't disrespect your elders.

Garret: Yes, Dad.

Alaric: I can be your daddy if that's what you want.

Garret: I guess you want to die and be buried next to the last Nox.

Alaric: After your next lesson in class, I think you'll want to save those thoughts for someone more deserving.

The thought of killing her sits like a hot coal in my stomach, burning my insides after she admitted the last thing I expected.

I imagined material things—money, an education, sex. It definitely wasn't the wish to die. Or for me to be the one to carry it out.

I'm practically running to class to find out what Alaric doesn't want to tell me over the phone. What's so *educational* that involves Rose?

The smell of her skin still lingers in my sheets. I snuck into the bedroom this morning while she was eating the breakfast I ordered. There was no way I could get rid of something that smelled so beautiful.

She reminds me of the lingering scent of a black rose. My little **Darkthorn.**

I knew if I touched her, she would consume me. And I couldn't let that happen.

I walk into my International Relations class and take the seat closest to the exit. I like the freedom to leave without making a fuss. Not like the professor would question me for ditching early, but still, I like to make things easy.

The fact that Alaric chose this class to tell me something doesn't sit right. International laws, globalization, human rights—nothing in this class should have anything to do with Rose. It's an easy course, one I took only because I had to stay my entire senior year when I could have graduated early and been sitting behind a desk, barking orders in my late father's building downtown.

I stretch my legs, ignoring the glances girls aim my way as they file in, staring at the time on my phone and waiting for class to start.

I only look up when the professor walks in—thick glasses, a porn mustache—waiting for him to announce that we have a *special guest*. My leg starts shaking.

Anxiety gnaws at me as Professor Mullen takes his time extracting a leather folder from his attaché. He notices me. Or maybe it's the tapping noise I'm making with my sneaker, repeatedly hitting the metal chair leg. I want to grab his head and shove it inside the damn thing so he gets the hint and hurries the hell up.

The door swings open, and my blood pressure skyrockets. Azriel. The last person I want to see. What the *fuck* is Alaric thinking?

Valen's younger brother doesn't belong in a place like this. He's good—better than most—but he's been doing questionable things lately.

Like caring too much for the girl who lied to us all. I see the way he looks at her. He *likes* her. Maybe he'd sleep with her if she showed any interest.

But I know she doesn't. She's still conflicted about whether she should trust him. And right now, she has every right to doubt him. Rose is an addiction for someone like me—a *psycho.*

I want to cage her.

Dominate her fucking mind.

Terrify her.

But at the same time, I want her to desire me.

She brings out the dark, unhinged version of myself that I keep locked away—the version I reserve for others when I want to wipe them off the face of the earth.

"Today, I want to go over human rights and globalization," Professor Mullen begins. "As you can see, I've brought Mr. Vikiar. He has conducted extensive research on the matter and would like to share his findings. This is an opportunity to spread awareness about the issue. He will cover human trafficking and the context of migration, labor, and exploitation."

Panic rises in my chest, forcing me to sit up.

Azriel's gaze lands on mine.

There's something in his eyes. Pity. Guilt. All I see is red. I want to strangle the knowledge from his mouth.

"My name is Azriel Vikiar. Some of you may not know, but I'm a hybrid student. I would like to share the results of my findings with you."

The class grows quiet. He shuts the lights. The projector flickers on. The bastard has a whole presentation prepared.

My eyes dart across the screen as he flips through images—buildings in the middle of nowhere. Then, an image stops me cold.

Young girls. Barely ten years old. They're dirty, malnourished. Their eyes hold a drug-induced daze—similar to the way I found Rose on the shower floor.

My stomach churns.

The bruises. The scars.

Track marks etched into their delicate skin.

Needles.

Drugs.

Girls sprawled on filthy mattresses in different rooms.

"This is where human traffickers hide their victims," Azriel says.

Gasps echo around the room. Some students watch with blank faces, unfazed.

It makes me sick.

"I know there are stories and reports of women and young boys being trafficked, but I would like to share this topic with children."

I only pick up bits and pieces of his words. The ones that matter. The ones Alaric *wants* me to hear. The ones that involve Rose. If that's even her real name. Because she might be nameless. No parents. Because these fuckers impregnate them to produce more. To sell them. Like animals.

Then I see it.

An image of a young girl with soulless eyes—

And a tattoo of a set of numbers.

I tear my gaze away. Bile rises in my throat, threatening to spill out of my mouth. No one knows what the numbers mean, but it's how they mark them.

To be used.

To be owned.

To be sold.

I bolt out of the chair. Rush into the men's bathroom. And throw up.

That motherfucker bought her like a dog.

CHAPTER FOURTEEN

"LET'S head to my dorm. We can get ready and then go to the party," Amy says with a smile as we exit our lit class.

I don't know how to tell her that the only decent outfit I have is a hoodie and leggings—the same ones I wore earlier this week. I really want to go, and in a way, I should make the most of my time before Garret comes for me. And it won't be just to tell me he has breakfast waiting in the kitchen.

He's been avoiding me all week. I hardly see him except when he feeds me and drops me off at school. The rest of the time, he's nowhere to be found. Not that I'm looking for him. Who would want to see the one person who is going to kill you?

Maybe he's giving me space.

There isn't much I can do.

"Um . . . I didn't bring any clothes to change into."

"No worries! I have something that would look great on you. I don't mind."

"Are you sure?"

No one has ever offered to let me borrow anything. I can't shake the feeling that I might be overstepping. I don't really know her that well—aside from the time we went to Babylon and our classes together.

"Yeah, I have this perfect dress with a black leather jacket that would look sooo cute on you." Her eyes sparkle with excitement, and I can't help but smile.

I check myself out in the bathroom mirror of the dorm

building. I look different. Amy applied eyeliner and a layer of foundation to my face. I'm wearing a tight dress with over-the-knee boots. I'm grateful for the jacket, but I'm unsure about showing five inches of thigh between the hem and the edge of Amy's heeled boots.

"Are you sure about this?" I ask nervously.

I've never intentionally dressed up for anything. The few times I had no choice were for reasons I prefer not to think about right now.

I'm sure Garret wouldn't care I didn't show up. But maybe he might. He never said I had a curfew or that I was obligated to wait for him after his swim practice. I simply didn't show up and ignored his last text asking where I was.

"You look gorgeous, Rose."

I catch Amy's red-lipped smile in the mirror's reflection. "So do you."

Amy is wearing skintight black jeans and a pink crop top that highlights her trim waist. Her strawberry-blonde hair is a cute contrast to her outfit.

As I shut the passenger door of the Uber—Amy insisted on paying for it—my legs shake. I watch the two red lights disappear down the road as the sun sets.

The volume of the music blaring from the house fluctuates, fading each time the front door opens and closes.

"Come on," Amy says, grabbing my hand. I stumble as she practically drags me toward the front door.

A couple of guys hold the door open with wide smiles when they see us. "Welcome, ladies," says the one with freckles, stepping behind us.

My internal radar kicks into full force as the smell of alcohol, heat, and perfume *hits me like a wave* from all the people crammed into the living room.

People dance to the beat of Kendrick Lamar's *Not Like Us*, singing the lyrics.

"Holy shit," Amy says over the music. "This is crazy."

A guy holding a keg of beer cheers while a girl underneath it tries to drink as much as she can, not caring that beer is pouring down her shirt—her nipples visible through the soaked fabric.

Two guys stand on either side of one girl as she takes turns French kissing them.

A ping-pong table is in the back. The girls are topless. Their breasts bounce harder than the ball every time they swing the paddle.

If this is an Ohio frat party, I can only imagine the type of party Garret throws. Orgies must be an understatement.

"Let's get a drink," Amy suggests, pulling me through the throng of people.

Curious glances follow me as Amy pushes through. They all must be from Ohio, because I have yet to see anyone from Kenyan.

Amy reaches the kitchen and grabs two beers from a bucket of ice. She pops the top off with a bottle opener and hands me one while she chugs the other.

A guy with light green eyes looks over. It's hard not to get lost in their bright depths. I'm not sure if it's a trick of the light. A guy with brown hair slaps him on the shoulder playfully.

Green Eyes nudges his head in our direction, says something to his friend, and they both head over.

"Do you know them?" Amy asks, taking another sip of her beer.

"No."

"They're kind of cute," she says. "They have to play football."

I understand why she made that assumption. These guys are not small by any means. They are big—with large hands and wide necks—the type that play football.

"Hey," Green Eyes says when he reaches me.

His friend watches Amy with interest.

"Hi," I reply a bit awkwardly.

I tune out Amy and the other guy. We stare at each other for a few seconds.

I'm not sure why he walked over, but all I can think is that he must want something. Or he's just curious. Recognition wraps around me like a blanket. It's like I've seen him before but never *really* paid attention.

My focus sharpens on the guy in front of me—his green eyes, the tiny freckles on the bridge of his nose. The way his mouth lifts higher on one side when he grins. He's not Garret by any means. He doesn't make my heart hammer in my throat. He doesn't make me wonder how it would feel if he kissed me. If I was the Darkthorn he called to make him bleed.

This guy is different in every sense. He doesn't know who I am. He doesn't look at me with disgust. He's looking at me like I'm human—a girl at a college party.

"Your name is Rose, right?"

How does he know my name?

Then his voice *digs the memory out.* The diner. The guy with the cowboy hat.

"Yes," is all I manage to say.

"I'm sorry about the other night. I didn't get to give you my name since we were so rudely interrupted."

He holds out his hand, and I take it, almost dropping my beer. If he notices, he doesn't point it out. His hand is rough but firm.

"I'm Leo. Short for Leonidas."

"Spartan!" his friend chimes in.

I arch a brow. Leo smiles. "My mom had a thing for the movie *300*."

I have no idea what he's talking about, but I nod. I've never watched the movie, but I don't want to sound clueless.

"Where's your cowboy hat?" I ask instead.

If anyone looked good in one, it would be him.

"You like the hat?"

"It's different. Kind of like your name."

His gaze drops to my beer, already getting warm. "Do you like beer?"

I shrug. "It's what everyone is drinking."

I tilt the bottle and wince at the bitter, lukewarm taste.

He chuckles, grabbing it from my fingers and tossing it in the trash. "Let's get you something that doesn't taste like piss." He flips the lid from a nearby cooler and hands me a Coke can. "I like my girl sober."

His words wrap around me like a warm embrace. For a moment, it doesn't matter that I have an ugly past. Or that after tonight, I will never see him again. He is a moment. Normal in all the ways I couldn't be.

So when he asks if I want to dance . . .

I don't hesitate.

CHAPTER FIFTEEN

GARRET

"YO, GARRET?"

I turn my head to the left. It's Clay from the team.

"What's up?"

I face the tiles, the hot water from the shower easing my aching muscles. I've been drowning out my conflicting emotions about Rose in the pool, punishing my body because there's no way I can look her in the eyes. I can't take the words back—the ones that replay in my head like a badly written song.

"You going to the Ohio frat party tonight?"

"Nah, man. I think I'll pass."

I continue to stare at the tiles, pretending to listen. The last thing I want is to go eat shit at an Ohio party. I texted Rose and almost flung my phone against the wall when she didn't respond. It's like I can't demand anything from her—not after what I learned.

"Some of us are going," Clay drones on. "Prey will be there."

Luke laughs. "Yeah, man. You don't want those fucks from Ohio to get dibs."

Some of the guys in Ohio are part of the Order. They don't have power like I do or like the sons of Kenyan, but they follow the same rules and are rewarded handsomely for it. They also have dibs on Prey, and the guys love to show them that we have the power to show up and do whatever the hell we want.

"Like that girl you bring to school," Clay says.

My vision narrows like I'm going through a tunnel. A loud sound goes off in my head, like nails on a chalkboard.

"What did you say?"

"That girl," Clay says, glancing at the other guys in the shower. Some look away. Luke swallows hard, his face almost healed from when I hit him after he talked about Rose.

"What about her?" I growl, shutting off the water and snatching my towel.

Clay's throat moves slowly as he swallows. "She went with that girl in her lit class. I overheard them talking about it in the hallway."

"Are you sure?" I press, imagining some asshole touching her, breathing in her scent, not caring if she wants to or not. Getting her drunk enough to sleep with her.

My vision goes red, the piercing sound of my rage boiling in my ears. I barge out of the shower, grabbing my bag from my locker, the metal door slamming shut like a cannon going off.

"What the fuck? Is everything cool, man?" Clay asks tensely. "Did I say anything wrong?"

Zipping my bag, I grab my hoodie. "No. Thanks for the heads-up."

I walk out and head to my car. The powerful engine roars as I press on the gas, but it's not loud enough to drown out the different ways this will end. They all have one thing in common: they end with me murdering someone.

I drive up the sidewalk, not caring if I fuck up my car. I park on the grass, over the pathway leading to the front door, and jump out, ignoring the gasps and wide eyes when they see me.

"Nice car, man," some idiot shouts.

I push open the door and scan the crowd. The moment I see her, the air grows thick. Her hands rest on the quarterback's shoulders. His fingers press into her small waist. Something sharp twists under my ribs. Clarity slices through the noise. I should leave. Pretend this never happened.

Instead, my vision clears. His hands don't belong on her. They should be pinned to the wall so the next asshole knows exactly what happens when he touches something that isn't his.

He says something to her. She tilts her head back and laughs. A knife lodges itself in my gut. It takes me a moment to recognize what I'm feeling. Something I should have buried with the rest of my mistakes.

Jealousy is a poisonous thing. Envy is the vine that feeds it, curling under my ribs, constricting until I can't breathe.

It's why she didn't answer my calls or texts.

"Hey, Garret! My man . . . you made it." Billy walks up, slapping me on the shoulder like he always does, oblivious to the way I'm feeling. "You check out my man Spartan? Since that night at the diner, she's all he talks about. The one that got away. The girl of his dreams."

He laughs. I want to deck him in the throat, but I don't. What would be the point? He has no idea what's racing through my head—how dangerous he and his friend are from being cut to pieces.

"I saw some of the girls out back."

He means the ones I mess with, but there's only one I

have my sights set on. And I'm the last person she wants to see.

"I'm not here for that."

Billy follows my line of sight, then his eyes widen. "Shit! Hey, man. Listen—in his defense, he didn't know. We don't want any trouble."

I can't blame Leo or Billy. This is my fault. I should've noticed the signs. But I failed. The same way I failed with Jess. With Veronica. And now with Rose. My pulse pounds as I watch her.

Still laughing.

Still touching him.

I flex my fingers and count.

One.

Two.

Three.

Then I move.

CHAPTER SIXTEEN

"YOUR NAME, ROSE. IT FITS."

"How come?"

I can't stop smiling. My face hurts from doing it so much. But I don't care. The things he says… No one's said them to me before and I don't want it to end.

"You're small. Delicate." He leans in like he can't get enough. "And you smell like flowers."

"You can thank the dollar store."

He leans back, giving me a funny look. "You're kidding?"

I shake my head. "I wish I was .But it's what I could afford."

"Well, it's smells nice."

"You're just trying to be nice."

He spins us around. "I don't joke about a girl and the way that she's smells."

I scan the crowd, searching for Amy. I find her smiling at his friend. Awareness creeps up my spine. My stomach clenches. I feel it before I see him. Garret.

He's watching me like a serial killer. Dark. Angry. He leans against the wall, arms crossed, eyes locked on mine. I wonder how long he's been standing there.

His gaze dips to Leo's hands on my waist. Suddenly, they feel wrong. Like flames burning my skin. Everything grows heavy.

"Is everything alright?"

I swallow hard, "I-I have to go."

Concern flickers across his face. "Why?"

"Because my ride is here." Is the only excuse I can come up with. He'll understand. Once he sees Garret.

"Where—"

"Times up, Loverboy," Garret cuts in, his tone sardonic.

Leo looks between me and Garret. "Oh, hey man." His tone is easy, but his eyes stay on me. "She doesn't need a ride. I can take her home."

"You want to come to my house?" Garret muses. Leo's brows pull together. "Because that's where she stays. It's where she sleeps." Garret pulls a joint from his pocket, lights it, and blows smoke in Leo's face.

"Garret…" I warn.

He holds up his hand. "Not yet, my little Darkthorn."

Leo swats the smoke away. "Is there something I should know?"

"Depends," Garret says, smoothly, the joint dangling from his lips.

Leo squares his shoulders. "On?"

Leo is about two inches shorter, but Garret but Garret is more intimidating More muscle. Tattoos. Darkness. More power.

"On what she wants to tell you." Garret grins. "I'll let her decide."

Bastard.

He's forcing me to walk away because we both know I can't tell Leo the truth.

"I'll see you later," I tell Leo.

He studies me. He must see it, that I have to go. That nothing he says will change my mind. "I'll call you."

I nod. gave him my number earlier, when we took a break to grab some water. We talked about his family in Texas. The ranch he grew up on. How is father is into oil.

He offered to show me sometime. Even if I knew that would never happen it was nice to imagine I could. Then Garret had to show up and ruin it.

"Alright," I say weakly, knowing I'll probably never see Leo again after tonight. I'm pretty sure Garret will make sure of it.

Leo leans in, aiming for a kiss on my cheek but Garret shoves him back. "Let's go." He grabs my hand, tugging, dragging me toward the exit.

"You didn't have to be such an asshole," I snap, yanking my hand free.

"I was saving you from heartbreak."

"How would you know? You don't have a heart." I pause, remembering I came with Amy. "My friend—"

"I ordered her a ride."

I blink.

"Told her she had to leave."

"Why?"

He shrugs. "Because I said so."

We step outside. I freeze. His car is inches from the first step. "Are you insane?"

He opens my door. "I think you figured put what I'm capable of." His voice lowers. "Even had glimpse with my friends." He holds the door. Waiting. Now, get in the car."

I fold my arms. "Or what?"

A shadow of amusement crosses his face. Then it disappears. He steps forward. His body cages mine.

I tilt my chin up. The back of my neck hits the edge of the door.

His eyes burn into mine. "I'll make sure our audience knows how wet you get when I press my cock over that hot cunt of yours."

Heat spikes up my spine. "You wouldn't." I challenge him. He smirks "I disgust you, remember?"

His eyes don't waver. They pin me in place. "Get in the car, Rose." Then he walks to the driver's side.

I don't move. I don't get in the car. Not until my pulse slows and my hands stop shaking.

CHAPTER SEVENTEEN

SINCE ARRIVING at Garret's house, he's been a ghost. The bedroom door was left open—a silent invitation, or maybe just indifference—but the space around me feels suffocating. Like the drive over here.

He didn't say a word. No cruel remarks. No taunts. No surprises.

Just silence.

He drove the short distance like I wasn't there. But that wasn't what unsettled me. It was the restraint. The tension.

Garret opened the car door for me, a gesture so unexpectedly chivalrous that I hesitated before stepping out. But that was as far as his civility went. No instructions. No threats. Just an unreadable gaze that sent a ripple of unease through my chest.

And now, I don't know how to feel. Am I angry that he dragged me away from Leo? That he ruined the brief glimpse of normalcy I'd let myself enjoy? Or am I conflicted by something else—that it *bothered* him? That he *saw me* with another guy and reacted?

I don't want to sit in this room and let my thoughts eat me alive.

Carefully, I push open the door and step into the hallway, my bare feet silent against the cool marble. The house is eerily quiet. No Ace. No sounds of movement.

I exhale, telling myself maybe Garret went to sleep. Maybe he left.

I move forward, curiosity leading me down a hallway —one I haven't explored before. The house is massive, a maze of intricate woodwork and cold stone, like a living museum of wealth and legacy.

I pass a library filled with books stacked to the ceiling, a ladder affixed to a rail. It reminds me of the one on campus, and for a moment, I pause, about to step inside.

Then I hear it.

A low splash, followed by another.

My heart jumps.

Music plays faintly, its haunting melody curling through the air like smoke. The intro of *No Time To Die* drifts through the open space, growing louder as I follow the sound. My pulse quickens when I step into the indoor pool area.

The water glows deep crimson beneath the submerged lights, sending ripples of red through the high-ceilinged room. Steam rises in soft wisps where the warmth of the pool meets the crisp night air filtering through the partially open roof.

And then, there's *him*.

Garret slices through the water with sharp, precise strokes, each movement smooth, controlled, devastatingly powerful. The muscles in his back shift with every stroke, his tattoos morphing like ink on liquid, his body moving like it was carved from stone.

I should leave.

I should turn around before he catches me watching.

But I don't.

My feet carry me closer, the marble beneath me cool and slick. I inch toward the edge, my breath shallow, drawn in by the mesmerizing sight of him—like a predator lost in its natural element.

The surface ripples hypnotically, lapping at my toes. I lean in just a little more, peering into the water, wondering how deep it is.

Then—

I *slip*.

A startled gasp escapes my lips, but it's swallowed instantly as I plunge into the water. A rush of warmth engulfs me, my body sinking, panic slamming into my ribs like a hammer. Water floods my nose, my throat, burning like fire. I try to surface, try to kick, but I can't find which way is up. The weight of the water presses against my lungs.

I can't breathe.

Then, a force like a wrecking ball collides into me.

A steel grip yanks me through the water in a powerful wave, and suddenly, I'm *airborne*. I choke, spluttering as my body is flipped onto its side, coughing up water while heat—warm, strong, *alive*—surrounds me.

"Rose! Fuck." Garret's voice is sharp, laced with something I can't name.

His arms are locked around me, his hand pressing against my back, rubbing slow, measured strokes as I struggle to breathe.

His touch is solid, grounding, his body radiating warmth as he holds me against his chest, keeping me *here*.

"Breathe," he commands, voice raw.

I do. A ragged, painful inhale that fills my burning lungs with precious air. I cough, my throat raw, my chest tight, but I *breathe*.

His fingers tilt my chin up, forcing me to meet his gaze. "You don't know how to swim?"

I shake my head weakly, still trying to process what just happened.

I could have drowned.

But he saved me.

"Why did you save me?" My voice is hoarse, barely a whisper.

His eyes flicker with something unreadable—something fierce. His grip tightens around me, his chest rising and falling like he just ran a marathon.

"You could have let me drown," I murmur, my voice hollow.

His expression darkens. His gaze drops—to my lips, to my throat, lower still, pausing just beneath the waterline where my soaked tank top clings to my skin.

When his eyes meet mine again, there's no hatred.

There's *fear*.

Before I can react, he shifts. His strong arms lift me effortlessly, my legs instinctively wrapping around his waist as he carries me through the pool. Water sluices off his skin, glistening under the dim lights.

I don't fight him.

I don't *want* to.

He lowers me onto the built-in ledge at the shallow end, the water lapping at my ribs. The cool night air brushes against my damp skin, sending a shiver through me.

His hand cups my cheek, his thumb tracing my jawline. His touch is gentle, contradicting everything I know about him.

"I'm okay now," I whisper, though my voice betrays me.

His gaze drifts lower. My chest rises and falls rapidly, my skin flushed from the heat of the water.

"Are you?" he murmurs, his tone unreadable.

I don't answer.

I *can't.*

Because the way he's looking at me—studying me like I'm something fragile, something *his*—makes my heart stutter.

I should pull away.

I should shove him back, remind him that I hate him, that I don't *want* this.

But I don't.

Because when he leans in, slow and deliberate, I realize I *do* want this.

To *feel.*

And Garret makes me *feel.* He makes me want to experience life another day.

His lips brush against mine—hesitant, waiting. *Testing.*

I don't stop him.

Instead, I fist my fingers into his shoulders, silently granting him permission.

A low groan rumbles from his throat as he deepens the kiss, his tongue sweeping into my mouth, claiming me with a slow, intoxicating rhythm. He tilts my head back, his hands tangling into my wet hair as he devours me, like he's trying to drown me in something other than water.

His mouth trails lower—to my jaw, to the hollow of my throat, his breath hot against my damp skin.

"Tell me to stop," he rasps against my collarbone.

I don't.

I *can't.*

Instead, I whisper breathlessly, "Don't."

His mouth crashes against mine again, hunger igniting between us like gasoline to an open flame.

My back arches into him, my body betraying every

rational thought in my head. His lips move lower, his hands mapping my body beneath the water, like he's discovering something forbidden, something he *never* planned to want.

I was breathless. His mouth devoured me—possessive, claiming, relentless. His tongue teased, his teeth grazed, and I could do nothing but surrender. There was nothing I wanted to think about except him.

He pressed against me, his body hard, unyielding. Heat radiated between us, searing through the thin barrier of fabric. Every deliberate roll of his hips sent a delicious shudder through me, and I arched into him, seeking more, needing more.

A groan rumbled from deep in his chest, primal and raw. His lips found my neck, and then—he bit me. The sharp pleasure sent a cry tumbling from my lips.

My fingers slid between us, wrapping instinctively around the rigid length of him. A bolt of heat shot through me, intoxicating and dangerous. And then he froze.

His breath hitched. His muscles trembled beneath my touch. His hands clenched at my waist like he was holding himself together by a thread.

"Run," he rasped, voice hoarse and strained, like the single word cost him everything. His throat worked as he swallowed. "Rose..."

The sound of my name on his lips shattered something inside me. I let him go like I'd been burned, my fingers tingling from the loss.

My legs slid down his hips, the heat between us cooling with the weight of reality pressing down on me. My heart pounded in my chest, the truth slamming into me with brutal force.

If I let this happen, what then?

I would be exactly what he said I was.

I staggered back, my breath coming in quick, uneven gasps. His gaze stayed locked on mine, dark and unreadable, but the tension in his body told me everything.

I had to leave.

CHAPTER EIGHTEEN

I BURY myself in the book I still haven't officially checked out from the library—sonnets, poetry, pieces of love and longing that feel like fragments of a world I'll never belong to. It's the only way to push away the memories of last night but at the same time it makes me wish it never ended.

The way his lips swallowed me whole. The way my body burned against his. The way I wanted it.

I don't care if I skip over words that are too difficult to read. I just need something to keep me from overthinking.

I brush my teeth and curl up on my bed, pulling my sweater over my knees. I don't have the courage to leave the room.If I go to the kitchen, I might run into Garret. And I have no idea how to face him—how he'll look at me.

Does this mean he likes me?

Does this mean he still hates me? The last thought makes my stomach churn, so I focus on the book, forcing my eyes over the words.

Then my phone chimes.

Leo.

> Leo: Good morning, gorgeous. I hope you haven't forgotten about me.

Guilt crawls up my spine, a million tiny ants swarming,

biting at my insides. I force a smile when another text comes through—this time with a cowboy hat emoji.

Rose: How could I? How many guys do you think I know that look good in cowboy hats?

Leo: I'm hoping it's just me. ;)

"Are you ready for your tutoring lesson?"

The deep voice makes me flinch. My phone slips from my hands, landing on the bed like a hot coal.

Garret stands at the foot of my bed, staring at the screen. At Leo's name. At the text.

He's shirtless.

Every sculpted muscle of his chest and abdomen is carved with shadows, disappearing beneath the band of his black sweatpants. His damp hair curls at the ends, fresh from a shower, the scent of his soap teasing my nose.

I swallow hard.

"Good morning," I murmur, my voice barely above a whisper. "I... I didn't think you were serious about the tutoring thing."

"You haven't eaten," he states, like it's fact, not concern. "I was waiting for you in the kitchen."

Warmth unfurls in my chest, slow and foreign.

No one has ever cared if I ate.

"I didn't think you noticed."

His eyes flick to my phone again before locking onto mine, his voice cool and unreadable. "I notice everything."

Heat spreads across my cheeks. Did he read Leo's texts?

I close the book, marking my place before pulling the hem of my sweater down my thighs. "I'll be right there."

But he doesn't move.

His eyes travel down my legs, stopping at my bare feet.

"You should wear socks," he mutters. "Or slippers. The floor is cold."

I blink. Garret doesn't care about things like that.

"I don't have clean socks," I admit quietly. "I don't own slippers."

His frown deepens. His gaze sweeps the room before landing on my backpack. The only thing I own.

"Do you want me to grab some clothes for you from the house?" He means John's house.

I shake my head. "What you saw in my dorm room? That's everything I own."

Something flickers across his expression, something I can't quite read. Without a word, he moves to the dresser, pulls open a drawer, and takes out a brand-new pair of socks.

"Sit." His voice is quiet but firm.

I hesitate, but my body obeys.

He kneels in front of me.

"What are you doing?" My voice is barely a whisper.

He looks up, his expression unreadable. "Making sure you don't get cold."

His fingers wrap around my ankle, warm and firm, as he pulls the sock over my foot. The oversized fabric slides up my calf, covering my skin. Then he does the same with the other foot, his touch surprisingly gentle.

I don't know how to stop the goosebumps trailing up my arms.

"Thank you," I murmur.

He doesn't respond, just stands and nods toward the door. "Let's go."

When I step into the kitchen, I freeze.

The island is covered with food—fresh pastries, soft bread, butter, muffins, colorful fruits arranged in careful rows.I've seen this spread every morning, but I always reach for the same thing.

Strawberries.

They're safe. Familiar.

Garret moves to the espresso machine, his broad back flexing as he grabs a cup from the cabinet. Effortless. Controlled.

He presses a button, and the scent of rich coffee fills the space.

Then, without turning around, he asks, "Do you want some?"

I stiffen.

"C-can I?"

He spins around to face me, his gaze locking onto mine. "Why would you ask me that?"

I swallow hard.

"Because I wasn't sure if I was allowed one."

His jaw tightens. "Have you ever had coffee before?"

I hesitate. Then shake my head. "No."

The espresso machine hums. The silence between us is louder.

Then, barely audible, he murmurs, "You like strawberries."

I nod.

"Is there anything you don't like?"

I glance at the pastries, my throat tightening. "Cinnamon."

His brows draw together. "Why?"

I fight the bile rising in my throat. "I just don't. It's disgusting."

He doesn't push. Just nods once. Then, without another

word, he walks over to the island and—one by one—starts removing selected pastries, cakes, and muffins.

My chest tightens. "What are you doing?"

"Making sure you don't eat something you hate."

I stare at him. "Why are you being so nice to me?"

He doesn't answer. Instead, he wraps the discarded pastries in plastic and slides them into the fridge. "For my housekeeper," he explains. "I'll make sure to order nothing with cinnamon."

I don't understand. After last night, something has changed. I don't know what to do with this version of him. "You don't have to go to all the trouble," I whisper.

Garret turns. Walks toward me. Lifts me off the floor.

"Garret!"

My stomach somersaults as he places me on the counter, stepping between my legs. His warmth presses into me. "What are you doing?"

He reaches for a square of pineapple, lifting it just before my lips. "Open."

The juice drips down his fingers, a golden trail glistening against his skin. Heat curls low in my stomach. I part my lips, biting the fruit from his fingers.

His gaze darkens as he watches me lick the lingering juice from my lips. "You like it?"

I swallow. "Yes."

His lips curve.

For the next thirty minutes, he feeds me, learning what I like, what I don't.

And for the first time—I feel seen.

CHAPTER NINETEEN

THE WEIGHT of uncertainty over Garret's motives dissipates as he settles beside me on the couch. He keeps a small distance, just like in the kitchen earlier, but not enough to stop the shiver from crawling up my spine or the goosebumps from appearing on my exposed thighs. If he notices, he doesn't show it. His gaze lingers but never for too long. He also doesn't mention what happened between us last night.

It's as if it never happened. As if he never threatened to kill me. As if he never decided, for reasons I still don't understand, that my life was worth saving.

"Alright, try this one," he says, pointing to a page in the book. "It's easier."

I glance at the poem—it's short. Manageable. I hesitate, taking a deep breath before beginning. The fourth word tangles on my tongue, and he corrects me gently. Patiently. I push through the rest, stumbling, fumbling—but he never makes me feel stupid.

"If you ever get stuck…" He unlocks his phone, pulling up Google Translate. "Type the word in. It'll help you pronounce it and show the meaning."

"Azriel told me I could look things up, but my phone doesn't work like that," I admit.

He flips the page. "I can fix that."

I glance at him. "How?"

"Don't worry about it." He nods to the book. "Try this one."

I lick my lips, reading the lines silently before daring to say them aloud. I don't push the issue about my phone. In the back of my mind, I keep waiting for him to snap out of whatever this is and go back to the way we were.

"Good," he says when I finish.

I laugh. "Are you kidding? I suck."

"No, you're just not used to it. But you'll get better. The more you practice."

I sigh. "I'll need a ton of books before I can read one page without tripping over my words. Half the time, I don't even know what they mean."

He chuckles. "Rose, there are plenty of people who don't understand what they're reading—people who read every day. They just pretend they do."

"But they're not in college, where it counts."

"I'll worry about that part. And I have a ton of books."

I glance at him nervously. "You wouldn't mind if I borrowed some?"

"I don't think anyone would object."

His fingers brush against my cheek as he tucks a strand of hair behind my ear. A tingling warmth spreads down my neck at the soft touch.

"You can have as many as you like," he murmurs. "You can go anywhere you want—except the pool." A gleam of amusement flashes in his eyes. "I think it's best you let me know if you decide to jump in again."

I smile shyly. "Probably a good idea."

———

A hot breath tickles my face, followed by a wet swipe across my nose.

I bolt upright, heart hammering.

Ace stares at me, his dark eyes steady, before laying his head back on my pillow like he belongs there.

"A little warning would be nice," I scold, wiping my nose.

He lets out a small whine.

I swallow hard, slowly reaching out to pet his head. He lifts it slightly, and I flinch, snatching my hand back.

"Don't show him fear," I whisper to myself.

Ace watches me. Waiting.

I exhale, repeating it again. "Don't show him fear."

Tentatively, I extend my hand once more.

He leans in.

The moment my fingers sink into his soft fur, I let out a triumphant little giggle. He licks my fingers, nuzzling into my palm, his massive head heavy against me.

"Good boy," I murmur, scratching behind his ears. He rolls onto his back, paws up, demanding a belly rub.

"He likes you." Garret's deep voice makes me tense.

I glance up to find him leaning against the doorframe, shirtless, his toned body bathed in the early morning light. I swallow, my mouth suddenly dry.

"I hope you don't mind, but I think he likes sleeping with you. He's protective."

I shake my head, still running my fingers through Ace's fur. "I don't mind. He scared me, but I think he's making up for it."

Ace lets out a satisfied groan, pushing his head against my palm.

"What would he need to protect me from?" I ask absently, scratching behind his ears.

Garret's expression darkens. "You never know. Maybe he doesn't like when you have nightmares."

I freeze.

I lower my gaze to Ace, my fingers slowing. My nightmares are nothing new. I've had them for as long as I can remember.

But if Ace was with me last night, watching over me…

Who else was?

"Did I keep you up?" My voice is quieter now.

Garret doesn't respond immediately.

After reading with him yesterday, I was exhausted. I don't even remember falling asleep. But I remember feeling warm. Safe. Wrapped in something I didn't want to wake up from.

I look up at him, our gazes locking across the room. And in his dark, unreadable stare… I know.

Ace wasn't the only one in my room last night.

CHAPTER TWENTY

AFTER SCHOOL, Amy begged me to come to Babylon to catch up. After the party, she assured me that Garret had gotten her back to the dorm safely.

"So, what is up with you and the swim team captain?" Amy asks, narrowing her eyes playfully over the rim of her beer.

"I should ask you the same about Leo's friend."

She waves a dismissive hand and takes a sip. "Friends. He's a player, and I'm not interested. I know the type," she says, her voice dropping on the last part. I catch the shift in her tone but don't push.

"There's nothing going on," I say, but even as the words leave my mouth, I know they're a lie. Not when I think about how Garret made sure I ate breakfast this morning—and how much I liked it. Not when I replay the way he opened every door for me as if it were second nature. The way he kept checking in on me on the drive to school, asking if I was okay, again and again.

"Didn't look that way to me at the party," Amy quips. "He practically threw you over his shoulder caveman-style when he saw you with Leo."

I shake my head. "He was just upset that I was avoiding him. His mom is married to the man who adopted me and… I'm also staying with him."

Amy's eyes go wide, her beer freezing mid-air. "You're kidding?"

"I wish I was."

Not many people know, but it was the only excuse I could give her. There's no way I could tell her the real reason I'm staying with Garret. No way I could admit that we kissed. That he saved me from drowning in his pool. That I liked it. That I still have the bite marks to prove it.

"How is he when you're alone?" she asks, lowering her voice. "I mean, he's always the life of the party, but he also has this dangerous quality. You know, 'don't let the nice act fool you' type of thing."

She isn't wrong. I thought I was the only one who noticed. But since that night at the party, Garret has me wrapped up in him. In his kindness. In the contradiction of him. And I can't get enough.

But he hasn't tried to kiss me again.

I thought it was guilt. Maybe regret.

I don't know what I'm feeling, but I can't ignore the way my body reacts when he's close. The anticipation of his touch. The way his gaze lingers in a room full of people.

And just when I convince myself it's all in my head, he does something that takes my breath away—like getting me a brand-new smartphone. Showing me all the features and how I could use it for my assignments. He didn't expect anything in return, just said it was a gift. A simple gift to help me out.

For the first time, I saw kindness in the dark depths of his eyes. A kindness I don't think he shows just anyone.

It felt like a rare gift—an eclipse of the moon.

I didn't know what to say, just thanked him over and over. And he just stared at me, his gaze deep, like he was committing the moment to memory.

"Is that why I haven't seen you in the dorms?" Amy asks.

I nod, wondering how many people had noticed. "Yeah. I don't know how he convinced his mom and stepfather, but I guess they agreed."

I leave out the part that he was ordered to take me in. That he didn't have a choice. Not that it mattered. No one goes against the Order.

And I still don't know if Garret's behavior is out of obligation. Or pity.

The bar grows louder as more people filter in. The sharp crack of a pool stick against a ball pulls my attention. My chest tightens when I spot a group of guys from the swim team—including Luke. But Garret is nowhere to be found.

I check my phone, but there's no text. Not that I expected one. He told me not to wait up for him after class.

"Do you know them?" Amy asks, catching me staring.

I snap out of it, shaking my head. "No."

She raises a brow. "Aren't they on the swim team with your boy?"

"He's not my boy," I say too quickly.

"He's not your brother either," she points out. "You're not related by any means. You didn't grow up together, right?"

"You sound like Garret. He says that all the time."

Her grin turns knowing. "That means he likes you."

I want to laugh at her assumption. Garret Nox might screw anything that moves, but liking me? That's something I don't think he's capable of.

I nod, wondering how many people have noticed the same thing. How obvious is it?

"Yeah. I don't know how he convinced his mom and stepfather, but I guess they agreed," I say, leaving out the part that Garret didn't have a choice. That he was ordered to take me in. It doesn't matter, though. Nothing could have changed it. No one goes against the Order.

And yet . . . I wonder if Garret's behavior is out of obligation. Or pity.

The bar grows louder as more people filter in, the air thick with laughter and the clinking of glasses. The sharp crack of a pool cue against the ball pulls my attention. My chest tightens when I spot a group of guys from the swim team—including Luke. But Garret is nowhere to be found.

I scoff, shaking my head. "He might screw anything that moves, but liking me? Not a chance."

Still, I keep checking my phone, hoping I didn't miss a message. Where did he go? There wasn't any swim practice today.

Last Sunday, he told me to take an Uber home and gave me the code to his house. Why? He was never this lenient before. He always had specific instructions—when to leave, when to arrive, when to wait. Now, suddenly, he trusts me?

Maybe it's nothing. Or maybe it's everything.

I can't stop the dream from creeping back into my mind.

Melody, a knife in her grip, stabbing wildly—but not at me. It was Melissa at the church. Then, another dream.

John.

I'm trapped in a dark room, my body frozen, terror rooting me in place. But then—there's someone else. A man in a mask. He saves me. But I don't know who he is.

"Where do you think he is?"

Amy's voice snaps me back.

"What do you mean?" I ask, though I know exactly who she's referring to.

A knowing gleam dances in her eyes. "You know who I'm talking about."

Before I can respond, a voice cuts through the din.

"Hey, ladies."

I glance up, and my stomach drops.

Luke.

Amy throws me a look—one that says, Why is he talking to you?

"Amy, this is Luke. Luke, this is Amy," I introduce half-heartedly.

Amy offers a weak smile, unsure how to react.

Luke barely acknowledges her before turning his attention to me. "I haven't seen you at lunch in a few days. You didn't answer my call about our date."

Amy arches a brow.

"I wanted to see if everything was okay," he adds.

I force a smile. "Oh, I'm sorry. I forgot Amy had asked me out first, so—"

"That's okay," he interrupts, but there's something off. A flicker of unease. His eyes keep darting toward the entrance.

I cross my arms. "I figured you'd understand. That's why I didn't bother to call. I'm sure there are plenty of other girls you've asked to come along."

I don't like how hard he's trying. I haven't given him a reason to pursue me, not even the slightest hint of interest.

Luke shifts awkwardly, running a hand through his hair. Silence stretches between us.

"I've heard you've been hanging around Garret," he finally says, rubbing the back of his neck.

My pulse spikes at the sound of his name. "Where did you hear that?" My voice is steady, but inside, I'm unraveling.

"I saw you two leaving after practice. It's been happening for a couple of weeks now."

Has he been watching me? Does he know John? Do the others know?

"Stalking is a crime, you know," Amy interjects, unimpressed.

Luke smirks. "It's not like I don't have eyes. Besides, everyone knows where Garret is—on campus and off."

Amy leans forward. "Oh yeah? Where is he now?"

I could kiss her for the way she asks it—like she doesn't give a damn, but like she knows I do.

Luke hesitates before shrugging. "I think he's with Cassie. They're off and on. You know how it is. Garret doesn't take anyone seriously."

A slow burn ignites in my chest, spreading like wildfire. I don't respond. I just stare at my beer, willing the words away. But they settle in my bones.Garret. Cassie. Of course.

Amy touches my arm gently, but I don't meet her gaze.

I feel sick. That night—the way he touched me, kissed me, made me feel wanted—it meant nothing. And I was stupid to think otherwise. When you've been shown cruelty your whole life, you cling to anything that feels different. Anything that makes you feel *human*.

I check the time on my phone, my fingers tightening around the device. I should throw it across the room. Should erase the reminder of him.

But I can't.

Because when you're desperate, when you have nothing, you don't let pride get in the way. It doesn't matter how much it hurts. Or who it came from. It's survival.

"It's getting late," I announce, glancing at Amy.

She understands instantly. "Yeah, we have a paper to work on," she lies, pushing out of the booth.

Luke gives me space to stand. "I guess I'll see you around?"

"Oh, sure," I murmur, my smile barely there.

We slip out the back exit, away from prying eyes. The night air is cool, thick with the scent of damp earth. Streetlights flicker, casting long shadows against the pavement.

A car door slams. I freeze. Laughter A voice. His voice.

Cassie walks ahead of Garret, her heels clicking against the wet pavement.

Amy must sense my hesitation, my urge to disappear. We stay hidden, watching as they round the building toward the entrance.

Garret isn't wearing the same clothes he had on this morning. Luke was right. He was with her. And that's why he told me not to wait.

A bitter taste fills my mouth. "Can I stay with you tonight?" I whisper, my voice barely there.

Amy doesn't hesitate. "Yeah, of course."

Garret doesn't owe me an explanation. We are nothing. But I can't face him tonight. Not after this. Not after realizing how foolish I've been.

I had one night. One fleeting moment where I let myself dream of something different.

He said my name like it was something precious.

He said I smelled like flowers.

He said I was beautiful.

CHAPTER TWENTY ONE

"ARE YOU GOING TO GET THAT?" Amy asks, shifting on her bed to face me.

Her dorm room setup is different from mine. She's on the third floor, in a space meant to be shared, but she doesn't have a roommate. There's an empty twin bed against the far wall, sheets folded neatly at the foot. She gave me a spare blanket, and though the room is small, it feels warmer than mine ever has. A tiny desk sits against the window, cork-board pinned with notes and photos, fairy lights strung above it like a halo, casting a soft glow across the walls.

It's the only light in the room.

My phone vibrates against the chipped nightstand, buzzing like it's possessed. The screen flashes with another missed call from Garret, followed by a series of texts.

> Garret: Where are you? You never made it home.

> Garret: Rose, answer the phone.

> Garret: ?

The screen lights up again, the glow hitting the ceiling like a flashlight in the dark.

I sigh, my fingers hovering over the power button. He could make me pay for ignoring him. Just like John. Garret acts like his house is my home, but I don't have a home. Never did. Never will.

He should have let me drown in his pool.

It would've been a perfect way to get rid of me—an accident, my own fault. Not at the hands of the people who have already planned my death.

I press the button, watching as the screen fades to black. A silent rejection.

I don't want to hear him threaten me. I don't want to listen to whatever excuse he has, don't want to see whatever expression he'll wear when I finally face him.

Not yet.

I drop the phone onto the nightstand with a thud—like shutting the final page of a book, a chapter closed.

"Don't want to hear it, huh?" Amy's voice is quiet, mirroring the storm inside me.

Anger. Regret. Defeat. Acceptance.

"What's the point?" I turn on my side, resting my head against my palm. "Thank you."

"For what?"

"For being a friend when you don't even know me. For letting me stay here."

She exhales, stretching her legs under the blanket. "I'm glad you asked. I hate being alone."

"Trust me, it's better than bad company," I say softly.

Amy hums in agreement. "Then you should surround yourself with better company."

"I am."

Her face lights up with the smallest smile, like I've given her something precious.

"Promise me something?"

"Anything," she says, her tone full of sincerity.

I swallow, my throat tightening. "When you graduate, find someone that makes you happy . . . after you land a job that lets you live in one of those apartments where you can see the stars and the city lights at the same time."

She laughs.

"And when you find that someone, make sure he tells you he likes your name, your smell, and that you're beautiful."

Her smile falters for the briefest second, sadness flickering in her eyes before she quickly masks it.

I wonder if she dreams of the same thing. I want that for her. Hope.Even if I don't get to live my dream, I can at least encourage her to live hers.I might not make it out of here alive. But she will.

"Why can't we do that together?" she asks, her voice tentative.

I can't tell her the truth. But I can give her hope.

"Yeah. Maybe we will. We just have to keep our heads straight and not fall for any of the assholes here."

She exhales, rubbing her palms together. "I don't get the best vibes from some of the people on campus."

I know exactly who she means. Luke. The others in class. The way they watch us. The stolen glances when they think we aren't looking.Like predators circling their prey.

"Same," I mumble.

What else can I say? That they want to use her? That they want to fuck her mind as much as her body? That they enjoy breaking people like us? That they bring girls here just to finish what our lives already started?

The next morning, I avoid large crowds and anyone who knows Garret. I steer clear of the places he hangs out, walking with my head down, adjusting the skirt and leggings Amy let me borrow. I'm grateful they fit—and that they're not as short as the ones most girls here parade around in.

I had been about to object when Amy pulled out the black pleated skirt and tights, but I didn't want to seem ungrateful. She's the only person I talk to, the only one I can sit in silence with who doesn't ask questions. It's like she's trying to break free from the chains of her past, while I'm desperately trying to escape my present.

But I know it's no use.

I can't run.

I can only dream—and hope that she'll be the one to live them.

For her. For me. For every poor soul walking through these dormitory halls, clinging to the illusion of a better life.

And me?

I just hope to live longer than the other girls who were in that room when John took me. I've heard the rumors—most of them don't make it. They die from overdoses, from trauma, from the beatings, or they simply disappear, never to be heard from again.

A breeze rustles through the trees, carrying the crisp scent of fall. My stomach growls, but I push past the hunger, opting instead for my favorite chips and a soda. I skipped breakfast—too afraid of running into Garret.

I find a spot near a tree by the church.

It's not really a church, but everyone calls it that—even though more people die inside than pray.

This spot is usually deserted. Amy's schedule doesn't align with mine on Tuesdays, so I eat alone.

"Keeping your phone off isn't smart."

Garret's voice slices through the breeze, making me jump. My bag of chips nearly spills onto the ground.

Fear curls in my stomach.

"Are you tracking me?" I ask, already knowing the answer. John did it. Why wouldn't Garret?

"Something like that." His tone is sharp, edged with restrained anger.

I sigh. "Can I finish my lunch before you do whatever it is you plan on doing?"

He steps in front of me, forcing me to crane my neck to meet his gaze. He's wearing a fitted sweater, black jeans, and dark sunglasses, but I can still feel his eyes burning into my skin, like the sun breaking through a cloudy sky.

"And what do you think I plan to do?"

"Kill me." I gesture toward the cemetery. "I can even show you the spot I picked out. It's far enough that no one will notice—or remember me."

He stiffens.

Despite the cool breeze, it feels like all the air has been sucked from the world.

The silence stretches between us, heavy, suffocating. The veins in his forearms flex as he clenches his fists.

Then, he kneels in front of me and pushes his sunglasses onto the top of his head.

His black eyes bore into mine, so intense it feels like lightning is about to strike.

"I'm not going to kill you."

"You're going against the Order?" My voice is flat, disbelieving.

"Let me worry about that."

"Then what is it you want?"

His answer is immediate.

"You in my house when I expect you to be. In my bed when it's time to sleep."

I swallow hard.

"I'm not fond of sleeping in your bed. It's a bit too crowded."

His jaw tightens, but I keep going.

"Besides, I gave you the night off from babysitting me. I thought you'd be grateful to spend time with Cassie."

Something flashes in his expression, but I don't stop.

"I was at Babylon last night. Don't worry, Luke cleared it up for me—and I saw for myself when you both arrived."

His face is unreadable, but his body is taut, coiled.

"What did you see?" His voice is controlled, but there's a sharpness beneath the surface.

I expected guilt.

But all I see is anger.

Why would he be angry? That I know what he was up to? That I think he's full of shit when he insists Cassie and he aren't serious?

"I saw what I needed to see," I say, my voice hollow. "I read what I needed to read in the messages you sent."

His jaw tightens.

"I'm just a puppet to you. A toy for your dog. I'm not important. So cut the shit and just get it over with. It wasn't like I didn't expect it."

I push myself to my feet, chin high, challenging him.

"You can drop the nice-guy act and be the monster we both know you are."

His nostrils flare.

His chest rises and falls with deep, measured breaths.

"Is that what you think?" His voice is low, dangerous, laced with something I can't decipher.

Anger seeps into his expression, into the hard set of his mouth, the rigid lines of his posture.

I brace myself. Because I know what happens next. I've seen it before. My reality is about to shatter.

And I'll be at the mercy of the monster.

"Let's go," he says with a finality that leaves no room for argument—like I'm a child who needs to be scolded for making the wrong assumption.

But I know what I saw.

I follow him to the parking lot, stopping when he halts in front of a sleek black Range Rover. I don't have to ask whose car it is—this is one of many parked inside his massive garage.

"You're driving."

I freeze in front of the hood. My panic must be written all over my face because he frowns.

"What's wrong?"

"I don't know how," I admit. "I don't have a driver's license."

His jaw tightens. "John really wanted you to be clueless, huh?"

Dumb is more like it—but at least he's finally catching on.

"Get in."

My eyes widen. "I can't."

Letting out a frustrated growl, he walks around to the driver's side, yanks the door open, and gives me a look that makes my stomach drop. "Get in the fucking car."

I don't argue.

As I step forward, he slides into the driver's seat and grabs my waist, lifting me onto his lap like I weigh nothing.

A gasp catches in my throat. The heat of his muscled thighs burns through my tights, igniting those damn butterflies in my stomach. My body betrays me every time he's near, and no matter how hard I try to push it down, the sensation lingers.

I tear my gaze away and stare at the massive screen on the dashboard. It reminds me of something from a spaceship I've seen on TV.

The car door shuts with a solid thud.

He presses his foot on the brake, pushes a button, and the soft purr of the engine fills the silence—along with my erratic heartbeat.

Then, his hands move. Slow. Purposeful.

Heat erupts across my thighs as his palms slide over the black tights stretched over my skin.

I squirm.

And that's when I feel it.

The hard length pressing against my ass—thick and growing by the second. "Keep squirming like that, and I'm going to fuck you in the school parking lot," he rasps.

I freeze.

My breath is trapped in my throat, my body betraying me again. My mind flashes to him flipping my skirt up, burying himself inside me, deep and rough.

Would I scream?

Would I like it?

Would I claw his eyes out?

No. I already know the truth.

I would let him.

Because Garret is not John. He is not David or the others. If Garret wanted to take me, he would have.

But he hasn't.

His need isn't about control—it's about me letting him.

And I did.

I let him kiss me.

I let him touch me.

I let him sink his teeth into my flesh and mark me.

And I didn't fight.

I didn't tell him to stop. I let him do things I never thought I'd let another man do—but him.

The shift in the air is suffocating, but he doesn't push me further. Instead, he places the car in reverse.

The screen shifts with a live feed of the rear camera, beeping softly as he maneuvers the vehicle with effortless precision. "This is reverse," he says, his voice calm, controlled. His large hands rest lightly over mine, guiding them to the wheel. "This is drive."

My fingers tremble beneath his.

"Relax," he murmurs against the back of my neck, his breath a dangerous caress. "I got you. You're doing great."

I forget that I'm sitting on his lap.

Forget the way he feels against me.

Because I'm driving.

A slow smile spreads across my lips.

"I'm driving," I breathe in awe.

It must sound childish, but I don't care.

I've wanted this for so long—for someone to show me I'm more than just a body.

"When you brake, press it slowly," he continues, guiding me. "If you stop too suddenly, someone tailing too close might rear-end you, or you'll be thrown forward. It happens, but only if you're trying to avoid hitting something—or someone."

A shiver runs through me. I tense, suddenly afraid of messing up.

His hands smooth over my thighs in slow, measured strokes.

Soothing. Grounding.

My leg shakes less.

We pull into an outdoor shopping mall. As the car rolls to a stop, a valet in a crisp red shirt immediately opens the door. "Welcome, Mr. Nox."

The valet's expression remains neutral, as if it's completely normal to see me sitting on Garret's lap.

"Park it in front," Garret orders. "I want my car ready when we're done."

We?

The word lingers. I don't think I've ever been included before. My pulse stutters. I've never been out alone with a guy before.

"What are we doing here?" I ask. "Don't you have class?"

"No," he says, unbuckling me like he does this every day. "And we're here to shop."

I blink, caught off guard.

I imagine he wants more things for himself—Garret never wears the same thing twice.

I've noticed.

His closet is the size of my entire dorm room floor—maybe bigger.

I wonder where he puts it all when he's done. Everything he owns is brand new—his socks, his underwear, his fucking bedsheets.

Always black.

Like his cars.

His kitchen.

His dog.

His heart.

CHAPTER TWENTY TWO

GARRET TAKES me into nearly every store.

I don't ask how much anything costs. I just stand there while he speaks with the clerks, watching the way their faces soften when they look at me—not because they care, but because he's buying something.

"She looks like a size two."

"I want the latest collection," he replies.

The woman behind the counter blinks slowly, reminding me of a sleepy cat. "Which one?"

Garret picks up a black leather boot embossed with two interlocking Cs in white.

"All of it," he says, as if she's new and doesn't understand his language yet.

Her eyes widen slightly before flicking to me. "Are you sure?"

Garret tilts his head and nods. "I'm sure. Also, if she touches it, add it. Spare no expense."

I swallow thickly. Did he just say he doesn't care how much everything costs? I lean over a nearby display, running my fingers over a small leather bag—one Amy would love. My eyes flick to the price tag.

Fifty-seven hundred. I snatch my hand back like it burned me.

"Do you like this one?" Joan—the store clerk, according to her name tag—immediately lifts the bag, eyes expectant.

I glance between her and Garret, panicked. "I was

looking for a friend, but I changed my mind," I say quickly, hoping to escape the moment.

"Get a new one. Gift wrap it."

I snap my gaze to him, stunned. Is he serious?

The corner of his mouth lifts in a slow, knowing smirk, and I swear my heart stops beating altogether.

By the time six rolls around, I want to collapse—preferably into the fountain at the center of the promenade. "How much did you spend?" I ask, panting slightly from exhaustion.

Garret laughs like it's nothing, but I know it isn't. His arms are loaded with glossy designer bags, the strings looped around his wrists like bracelets. Every time I offered to carry something, he refused.

"A lot," he finally says.

"How much is on that card?" I press.

"There isn't a limit."

I stop walking. "What?"

I've never heard of a card without a limit. Whenever I tried to buy something and miscalculated in my head, my card would decline. "That's not possible."

He shrugs, unbothered. "It's not going to be a problem for you anymore."

My stomach clenches. He makes it sound so simple— like I'm his responsibility now. The moment I've been dreading all afternoon finally arrives.

I inhale deeply. "How can I pay you back?"

Every store he walked into, he dragged me along. Every luxury brand, every exclusive collection, he bought it all. Shoes. Clothes. Perfume. Handbags. Silk underwear. His SUV is stuffed to the brim, overflowing with shopping bags.

He spares me a glance, then effortlessly shifts the car

into drive. "I want you to smile. That's how can pay me back."

My insides melt into liquid fire.

A smile. That's all he wants in return.

I was so sure he was evil, but now… I hope he's not.

The next day, the hope doesn't last long.

I see it before I even step onto campus—the flashing red and blue lights, the cluster of news vans parked in disarray, the yellow crime scene tape stretched across the quad. The main entrance is blocked off. Cops won't let anyone through.

I don't know who did it. But I have a very good idea.

Luke was found nailed to the cross outside the church —upside down, naked. His eyes were missing. His tongue was cut out. The words "A LYING TONGUE IS A PERSON WHO SEEKS DEATH" were carved into his chest.

I shudder violently.

The police are asking questions, but they don't have any leads.

I do.

Because I know who could have done it. And why.

Garret.

I don't know how I know, but I do. It was Luke who told me about Garret and Cassie. It was Luke who made me confront Garret. It was Luke who couldn't stop looking at the door that night in the bar.

Amy rushes up to me in the hallway, breathless. "Did you hear about Luke?"

People are crying. A makeshift memorial is already set up on campus—flowers, pictures, candles.

I nod, but her expression tells me everything. She knows—or at least, she suspects. "Yeah, it's crazy," I say. "One minute he was there, and the next, he…"

"Got nailed to a fucking cross," Amy supplies. "I wasn't fond of him. He was a little pushy, but shit… that's a fucked-up way to go."

My stomach twists violently.

What if Garret changes his mind about me?

"Hey."

I turn around. Garret is standing there, watching me with soft, careful eyes—like nothing happened. Like today is just another normal day.

"Hey," I reply, wrapping my arms around myself, suddenly grateful for the new sweater he bought me.

He leans in, pressing a kiss to my cheek, and I swear my toes curl inside my new designer boots. "Did you give your friend her gift?" he asks, expectantly.

Amy perks up. "She did! I keep asking if she won the lottery."

Garret smiles—a slow, knowing curve of his lips, like the cat that got the cream. "I think she did. She just doesn't know it yet."

My stomach tightens. What the hell does that mean?

"Anyway," Amy chimes in. "I hope you don't mind, but I'd like Rose to hang out at the Babylon tonight. My treat."

I glance between them.

Amy is waiting for his permission.

Garret smiles, but it's calculated—like he's plotting something. "Sure," he says, sliding his hands into his pockets. "I'll meet you there."

"Okay."

Before I can react, he presses a second kiss to my neck—lingering just long enough for his teeth to graze my skin. I swear I feel him smile.

He walks away, completely unbothered, as if he didn't just claim me in front of everyone.

"Damn," Amy mutters, watching him go.

"What?"

"That boy is crazy about you."

I almost burst out laughing. *If she only knew.* "Why do you keep thinking that?"

"You should see the way he looks at you. When I asked if we could hang out, he wanted to murder me for taking you away."

I shake my head. "You're imagining things. We both saw who he was with, remember?"

Amy doesn't look convinced. But deep down, neither am I.

Because something about what Luke said doesn't add up. And now, Luke is dead. His body was carved with a message.

A LYING TONGUE IS A PERSON WHO SEEKS DEATH.

Was it Garret's way of telling me Luke lied?

Or was it a warning meant for me?

———

Instead of Babylon, Amy decides we should go somewhere else.

We take an Uber across town to a dive bar near Ohio State. The place is smaller than Babylon but looks bigger from the outside. Inside, it's evenly spaced out with a rustic, lived-in feel—mismatched tables and chairs, two pool tables, an area for darts, and a bar positioned at the center. The music isn't bad either, probably because people pay to hear what they want.

"I thought we needed a change," Amy says, sliding into a booth just as Timeless starts drumming through the speakers.

I text Garret to let him know. I don't bother sending the address—I know he'll find me anyway. The tracker he has on my phone makes sure of that.

Except for the night I stayed in Amy's dorm.

I have a feeling he knew, but he didn't mention it. That's the thing with Garret—he's quiet. Unpredictable. I never know what he's going to do or what his motives are.

The thought of Luke still lingers in my mind.

I should feel bad. I should feel remorse.

But when you've lived around death for as long as I have, when you've been surrounded by people who do nefarious things, a dead body isn't shocking.

It's a norm.

I've seen worse.

Amy stiffens suddenly, her eyes widening. "Oh my God."

"What?"

"Don't look now, but that guy—Leo? He's here. Right behind you. Playing darts."

My spine stiffens.

Slowly, I turn over my shoulder.

Leo's laughing with one of his friends, smiling as he bends to pick up a dart from the floor. His shirt clings to his broad chest, the words OHIO FOOTBALL printed across in bold white letters.

Our eyes connect.

Shit.

I whip back around, praying he didn't notice me.

"Shit," Amy mutters, lowering her head. "He's coming this way."

"Hey, beautiful. Aren't you going to say hi?"

Leo's grinning down at me, easygoing as ever.

I hadn't expected him to walk over. He hasn't called or texted my other phone—not once.

I check it every day, but not for him.

For John.

And deep down, I have a terrible feeling that one day, he's going to show up.

That I'll have to pay for staying with Garret.

Or worse—he already knows my fate.

And he's simply stopped caring.

"Hi," I say, forcing a polite smile. "I didn't want to bother you when you were busy with friends."

Leo leans against the booth, bracing his hand against the top of the seat behind me. His smile deepens, cocky and sure. "You could never bother me."

Amy's brows shoot up at his confidence, but then her gaze shifts past him, locking onto something behind me.

My stomach drops.

I don't have to turn around to know. I sense him before I smell him—Garret's exotic cologne drifting through the air.

"You're in my way," Garret says scathingly.

But he's not alone.

Leo straightens, stepping aside to let him through. He doesn't expect Garret to slide into the booth right next to me, nor does he expect the seething glare Garret sends his way. I barely have time to process before my eyes shift to Azriel, who's standing beside him.

His gaze flickers between Amy, me, and Leo, assessing the situation. "Aren't you going to introduce me to your friend?" Azriel asks, his gaze trailing over Amy's face—

lingering a little too long on her chest—before snapping back up to her eyes.

Whoa.

I've never seen him act this cocky before.

Amy's face flames bright red.

"Amy, this is—"

"Azriel," she cuts in, rolling her eyes dismissively. "I know. I tried signing up for tutoring once, but he said he was too busy."

Azriel doesn't flinch.

"I was," he replies dryly before turning back to me.

"Are you okay?"

His eyes narrow playfully, but I know what he's really asking.

I meet his gaze with a knowing smile. I see what you just did.

Azriel's protective instinct is kicking in.

I like him, but I know where his loyalty lies.

And Amy? She's Prey—just like me.

"Hey, man."

Leo claps a hand on Azriel's shoulder, greeting him like an old friend.

Azriel doesn't so much as blink. He merely lifts his chin, utterly indifferent.

Leo doesn't take the hint.

Instead, he slides into the booth next to Amy, making himself comfortable.

Azriel's jaw tics, but he doesn't say anything.

A small smile tugs at my lips.

"Aren't you abandoning your friends?" Azriel asks, gesturing toward Leo's crew across the bar.

Leo doesn't miss a beat. "They're fine."

I swallow hard as my eyes dart toward Garret.

He's watching Leo like a predator. Unblinking. Seething.

Leo, for some reason, seems immune to the death glare currently directed at him.

Then, just to fucking test fate, he smirks and winks at me.

"Wink at her one more time, and I'll rip your eyelids off."

Garret's voice is low. Deadly.

"That's your only warning."

"Garret—"

But before I can stop him, he yanks me out of the booth. Drags me outside.

Pushes me against the brick wall of the building.

The sun dips below the horizon, casting the alley in shadows.

Time slows.

His body presses against mine, heat radiating through my clothes.

"Because you're mine," he growls.

Before I can speak, his lips crush against mine.

I gasp—and he takes advantage, plunging his tongue deep into my mouth.

His hands grip my thighs, lifting me off the ground, and I wrap my legs around his waist without thinking.

"Mine."

He squeezes my ass, his fingers digging into my flesh.

"He doesn't get you," he murmurs between kisses.

"I get you. I want you. I need you. I'll save you, Rose."

His words are a promise. A plea. A curse.

"What's it going to take, huh?"

His breath is ragged. His hands shake with restraint.

"For you to see it?"

I can't think.

I can't think when he's like this—dark, feral, unhinged. When he presses his cock against me, rolling his hips so I feel exactly how hard he is. "What about—"I start, but he cuts me off.

"I'm not with her. I'm not with anyone. Can't you see, Rose?" His voice is wrecked. Desperate. "I can't be with anyone else. I can't come with anyone else." He bends his knees, grinding against me. "Feel that...my little Darkthorn. His dick is big and hard pushing between my black leggings. The rubbing my clit. "Fucking feel that?"

My head spins.

"I have to beat you out of my dick knowing you're sleeping in my bed every night." He presses harder. I ache. "Do you know what that's like?"

My body wants him but my mind doesn't understand logic. It only understands him and his words. "I want to fuck you, but I can't. Not until you want me. Not until you say yes. Because I can't hurt you, Rose. I'll die...I'll die knowing you're not breathing."

I don't stand a chance. I know it now. I'm falling for him.

CHAPTER TWENTY THREE

GARRET DRIVES like a madman through the streets of Kenyan, his grip tight on the wheel, the low growl of the sports car vibrating through my bones. He doesn't speak. Not once.

When we reach the house, the doors swing up, and he's rounding the car before I even unbuckle. His hands find me, lifting me effortlessly as if my hesitation doesn't exist.

Azriel assured him Amy would make it back to the dorms. I wasn't worried. Azriel, despite being a son of Kenyan, has a heart. He wouldn't hurt Amy. But I don't trust him with her heart.

Garret makes a sound of frustration at my sluggish pace and picks me up, carrying me through the threshold and straight to his bedroom. I don't have time to think. I barely have time to breathe. He sets me down on the bed, stepping back only long enough to pull his shirt over his head.

My mouth goes dry.

He's perfect. The hard planes of his muscles flex beneath inked skin, each tattoo an untold story. Thorns curl over his heart, inked deep. Dark and possessive.

His gaze locks onto mine ."Tell me," he rasps, voice rough with want. "Is this okay?"

He's asking for permission. Tears sting my eyes.

His expression tightens when he sees them. "Don't cry, Rose. I'll stop."

I shake my head, pressing my lips together to keep my

emotions in check. "No, please. Don't," I whisper. "I'm just... happy."

His brows furrow slightly, as if he's trying to decipher whether he's hearing me correctly. "Are you sure?"

I nod, breath hitching.

His jaw flexes, shadows darkening his features. "I'm not gentle, Rose. It's why I've tried to stay away. I've tried to keep my distance, but once you say yes..." His voice drops, guttural. Dangerous. "I'm going to fuck you. I'm going to fuck every man from your memory."

Shame burns through me at his words. The memories—the past I can never erase.

"I know how you got your tattoo."

My breath falters. The pieces click together. That's why he changed.

His hands slide up my thighs, his thumb pressing against my clit, sending a shockwave of pleasure through my body. His tongue darts out between his lips, wetting them as he watches me.

"I'm sorry I judged you," he murmurs. "But I don't regret shaving your pretty pussy."

A strangled gasp escapes me as I press my hand over his, pushing harder against the pressure of his thumb.

"Fuck, Rose," he grits, the muscle in his jaw contracting.

Heat pulses between my legs, an unbearable ache. My body betrays me, hips rolling in a slow grind against his hand. He watches me come apart for him.

His fingers find the band of my leggings and tug. He slides them over my hips, down my thighs, stripping me bare, tossing them behind him. His eyes flick to my panties —silk, thin lace, already wet.

His nostrils flare, dark hunger twisting across his face. "I can smell you," he breathes, voice thick.

"Then let me feel you."

His lips part slightly, eyes flicking up to my sweater. His fingers find the hem, and I let him pull it over my head. My bra follows.

He moves slow, calculated. Holding himself back. I know he wants to tear my panties away, to claim me completely—but I make him wait. Because this moment isn't just sex.

It's ours.

"I've made a lot of mistakes in my life, Rose," he murmurs, stripping the last barrier between us. His cock stands proud, thick and heavy, silver barbells piercing from tip to shaft. He strokes himself, watching me watch him.

He's beautiful.

"But you…will never be one of them," he says.

His words shatter me. Because I know what it feels like to be a mistake. I've spent my whole life feeling like one.

But as he kneels between my thighs, inhaling me like I'm the only thing he's ever wanted—I believe him.

"Fuck," he whispers, voice wrecked. "You smell so good." His head dips, the flat of his tongue dragging over the lace, over the heat of me.

Pleasure explodes through my body like a wrecking ball. My nipples tighten, aching. My legs tremble as my breath stutters out in a desperate moan.

"Garret…" I gasp. "Please… more."

He smirks wickedly, straight black hair falling over his brow, his pitch-dark eyes, the white part visible glinting up at me like the devil himself. Then, he flicks his tongue. A strangled sound rips from my throat. He doesn't stop.

He grips my hips, holding me in place as I writhe beneath him. My hands fist the sheets, my body arching into him as pleasure tightens in my core. I want him to rip the lace but I break.

My climax crashes through me, a scream tearing from my lips as my vision blurs. My body convulses, tremors rolling down my legs as wet heat floods me.

Garret groans. He rips my panties off. Clamps his mouth over me. Drinks me in.

I'm still gasping when he rises, fisting his cock, pressing the tip against my slick entrance. My heart stutters at the delicious pressure, my body aching for more.

Our eyes lock.

I don't look away. I don't blink.

He pushes inside me. A strangled cry escapes me, my thighs trembling. One of his hands flattens against the mattress by my head; the other grips my leg, holding it over his hip.

He moves. Slow. Deep. Hard. Raw.

His gaze never leaves mine. Consuming.

His jaw clenches. "I didn't use a condom," he rasps.

I know. I can feel everything.

"I'm clean," he adds, voice tight, rough. "But I'm coming inside you, Rose. Do you understand?"

I nod, breathless. "I'm on birth control."

A wicked smile curls his lips. "Okay." He flips me onto my stomach, pulling my hips up, slamming into me from behind.

A shocked moan escapes me as his fingers tangle in my hair, pulling my head back. His teeth scrape over my shoulder, his tongue soothing the bite.

"You're so fucking beautiful," he groans. His hands roam—skimming over my breasts, teasing my nipples as his thrusts slow, deep, measured. He rubs his nose over my cheek, breathing me in. "This pussy," he growls, thrusting harder. "Is fucking *perfect*."

I cry out, gripping the sheets, lost in the rhythm of him. His lips find mine, devouring me as he fucks me—owns me. His thrusts turn frantic. His body tightens.

"Fuck—Rose, I'm gonna come."

His words slur against my lips, his voice desperate, wrecked. His movements become erratic, his fingers digging into my hips, his cock pulsing—hot, thick, endless. My body clenches, milking him.

He keeps moving. Keeps fucking me. Keeps worshipping me.

His arms wrap around me as he rolls us, my back pressed to his chest as he fucks me slow, lazy, deep—like he never wants to leave.

Billie Eillish's *Lovely* plays through the house speakers as he kisses my neck, whispering words against my skin. "You're perfect, Rose." His breath skims my ear, fire erupting in its wake. His hand presses over my heart. "I promise," he whispers. "I'll never let anyone hurt you."

I turn my head, catching his lips. And for the first time…

I believe him.

CHAPTER TWENTY FOUR

GARRET

"I HEARD you've been spending time with a Prey around town," Draven's father says, lighting a cigar.

The other members of the Order watch me, waiting for a reaction. The old man is bringing it up to make a point—Rose is off-limits. It's been three weeks since I first tasted her, and I can't get enough.

"I have," I admit easily.

John shifts in his seat, his anger a live wire beneath his skin. He watches all fifty members in their respective chairs but says nothing. He knows better. Someone else needs to take his place—someone more deserving. Because John Strauss doesn't deserve to sit here. He doesn't even deserve to breathe for what he's done to my girl.

I scan the room, noting the familiar faces. All members of the Order are present, but there's one other person I'm interested in seeing. Leonidas, he looks away but he's getting it now.

"Nice piece of ass," Alaric's grandfather comments, exhaling a slow puff of smoke.

I let it slide.

He must have helped Alaric uncover Rose's past, so I'll let him talk. He doesn't mean anything by it, and I can't blame him.

Rose does have a nice ass. And I've been fucking that ass all night, every night.

Still, baby steps.

She needs to trust me before I introduce her to my darker tastes.

John grunts. I turn to him, my glare cutting like a blade.

"Problem, Strauss?" I ask, my voice deceptively calm.

"She's not yours," he states triumphantly, his chin lifting.

I smile.

I can see the flicker of uncertainty in his gaze.

"Right now, my DNA dripping between her thighs says otherwise," I shoot back smoothly.

Laughter erupts around the table. The twins, Reid, Valen, and Alaric throw their heads back, their amusement filling the boardroom. Even old man Bedford chuckles. They all know what I mean.

Touch her, and I'll kill you.

Clearing my throat, I shift my focus. "I have a matter to discuss." My eyes flick to Valen, then to his father. Old man Vikiar is going to be pissed. But I don't give a fuck.

It's time.

"What is it?" Alaric's grandfather asks, the room quieting as all eyes turn to me.

"There's one son missing from this table," I state, my voice measured but firm. "He needs to be here. It's his birthright."

"How dare you?" Valen's father spits, his face going red, like he's seconds from a heart attack.

The other elders glance at him, some raising their brows at his outburst. He quickly composes himself, adjusting his tie with a forced calm. Then, begrudgingly, he concedes.

"Yes, but he's right." Alarics's grandfather turns to me and Valen, reluctant but resigned. "Next meeting,

Garret. Valen. Bring him. He needs to be here, as his birthright."

A slow smile spreads across my face.

Finally.

But John isn't done.

"And the issue with the girl?" he prods, his voice sharp. "The Prey."

I flick my gaze to the piece of shit across the table. I wish I could end him now—but patience.

"What about her?" Bedford asks through a slow drag of his cigar, the smoke swirling like a raincloud above his head.

"He has to let her go if he can't do what was asked," John insists.

Reid's gaze sharpens. I know exactly what he's thinking. *Kill him now and get it over* with. His eyes dart to mine. I give a subtle shake of my head.

Not yet.

I have a plan.

I've had one since Rose first arrived. I hated that she lied, but I knew something wasn't right. Valen knew too. But we didn't have proof—until now.

John bought her. The Order doesn't condone human trafficking. Children are off-limits. It's messy. Disgusting. But we still need evidence. Not that it matters—John doesn't get a free pass. He's already dead.

I promised Rose. I promised myself when I first laid eyes on her, when I first heard her snarky mouth. Rose was mine before she even knew she was.

"She's chosen to stay, John," I remind him. "She's a student on campus. You know the rules. Besides, why do you care?"

"I'm her guardian," he sneers.

"She's an adult."

"Who's going to provide for her?" he challenges.

I will.

I have.

"It's no trouble for Garret," Bedford cuts in. "He has more money than you." He leans back, tapping ash from his cigar. "Find another woman to park your dick in, John. I'm sure Mary won't mind. Buy her a Rolls and a trip to the Maldives. She'll look the other way."

I let the jab at my mother slide. Everyone knows how I feel about her.

I don't give a fuck.

"Let it go, John," Draven speaks up, scrolling through his phone. He's bored, itching to get back to Gia and the kids.

John doesn't take the hint.

"So, does anyone have anything to say about Luke?" he asks, bringing up the real reason we were called here. "The boy's father is distraught."

"He shouldn't have stuck his nose where it didn't belong," I say flatly, my tone devoid of emotion. "He was warned, John. Drop it."

John snaps. "You son of a bitch!" he roars, lunging out of his seat.

I grin. "You're not wrong," I reply lazily. "But then again, you married her."

The chair behind him topples over, slamming against the floor-to-ceiling window.

Silence blankets the room.

Reid sighs, shaking his head. "Pay him," he says simply. "If he starts any trouble, the Consortium will take care of it."

We all know what that means. We'll take care of it.

John's face twists in rage, but he knows he's lost. "You won't get away with this," he spits before storming out of the boardroom.

Coward.

"Handle it," Old Man Caruthers orders. "The girl is your responsibility, Garret. Do what you want with her."

His tone leaves no room for debate. "Alaric already briefed me." Then, he lowers the gavel. The meeting is over.

We all rise.

Valen's father turns to him, eyes filled with fire and hate. "He's your responsibility now," he seethes. "You got what you wanted." Then, he storms off.

Valen meets my gaze. Azriel is officially a son of Kenyan. But people don't know the truth. As nice as they think he is, there's a part of him his father doesn't want the world to see.

He's a patient from the fourth floor.

And someone had to help me nail that fucker to the cross.

CHAPTER TWENTY FIVE

FOR THE THIRD time this morning, I retch into the toilet, my stomach twisting violently. My nose runs, snot dripping, as I clutch the rim, feeling like my insides might spill out through my mouth.

Leaning back against the cold tile wall, I wipe my mouth with the back of my hand, sweat slicking my brow. My ribs ache from the force of vomiting. Maybe I ate something bad. Or maybe I caught a stomach bug.

I exhale shakily and glance at the small teak table near the sink, where a folded note waits for me.

Garret's handwriting. My heart clenches. He was the one behind the first note. Who would've thought Garret Nox was a romantic?

Smiling softly, I pick up the letter, pressing it to my chest. I love him. The forever kind. The kind that roots itself so deeply inside you, no one could ever measure up.

He's embedded in me like vines creeping through cracks, wrapping around my heart, refusing to let go.

I unfold the letter, my pulse pounding as I read:

You have broken the darkness around my heart with a kiss.
Your warmth, the scent of your skin.
The essence that is you.
It is only you that it beats for,
When death comes knocking, I'll answer.
I'll surrender.
To save the Darkthorn I bleed for.

I press the paper against my chest. Still lost in my

thoughts, I pad toward the kitchen, craving something light to settle my stomach.

But the moment I hear laughter, I freeze. A woman's laughter. A sharp, ringing sound puncturing my ribs.

Then, his voice—low, amused. Laughing with her. Jealousy spikes through my veins.

Steeling myself, I step forward. Garret stands shirtless, smiling at a woman—a woman so stunning she could crush me with a glance.

Long, inky-black hair cascades down her back, skimming a slim waist and wide hips. Her lips full, glossy curve in a knowing smile.

She's been with him. I can tell.

She lifts a delicate hand, feeding him a bite of cake from her fingers.

The intimacy of it makes my stomach churn. I no longer feel hungry. I no longer feel anything but a sick, twisting knot of realization: This isn't new.

The way they stand too close together. The way her manicured nails brush his wrist as he takes the bite. The way her dark eyes drink him in. Playful. Too friendly.

She isn't Prey.

She isn't like me. Her dress is designer—black, mid-thigh, expensive. She belongs to his world.

"It tasted better last time I made it," she says, solidifying my thoughts.

Garret grimaces, chewing slowly. His expression shifts. "It tastes... off." He shaking his head. "Not good enough."

I clench my fist so tightly I don't realize I'm still holding the note.

Her eyes find mine.

I look away in defeat.

I move toward the trash can, wave my hand over the sensor, and crumple the note into a ball.

Garret steps back from her, but not far enough.

"Hey..." He clears his throat. "Did you sleep well?"

The black steel lid lifts.

I force a smile. "Yeah." I drop the note.

The lid closes.

"Hungry?" he asks.

I shake my head. "Not really."

I don't look at him.

Instead, I turn to her. The woman he didn't introduce me to. The woman he let feed him. "Hi," I say smoothly. "I'm Rose."

Her smile is perfect. "It's nice to meet you," she says. "I'm Veronica." Then she glances at Garret.

Veronica. Even her name is beautiful. A perfect, glossy, effortless Veronica.

I glance at the cake. Garret never asked me to bake for him. Granted, I don't know my way around a kitchen. But I would have tried.

I would have learned. I would have done anything for him—if only he had asked.

But he asked her.

He was here with her while I was upstairs, puking my guts out. He didn't even know.

The tension thickens. It smothers me like a heavy fog. I know Garret has a past. And I know mine isn't pure. But watching him parade it in front of me—or worse, knowing he might still be fucking her, rips something apart inside me.

We never talked about what we are to each other. I was stupid to think I was special. Garret can have whoever he wants. Why would he waste his time with me?

A wave of nausea rolls through me. My hands turn clammy. My stomach lurches. I need to get out of here.

Garret grabs a plate of strawberries. "You sure?" he asks.

Veronica smiles and plucks one from the plate. "Aww…you remembered?" she says, softly.

Acid burns my throat.

"I try," he says, as if I'm not even in the room.

I swallow hard and clear my throat. "I'll leave you two to finish."

Veronica hesitates. "Oh, I can go—"

"No, stay." I force my best fake smile. "He invited you." I lie through my teeth. "I have a paper due. You can keep him company." I turn away before my voice cracks.

"Rose?" Garret calls.

I pause. I don't turn around.

Tears silently streak down my cheeks. "Yeah?"

His voice is soft. "Call me if you need help."

I nod, swallowing the lump in my throat. "Yeah. Of course."

I make it to the bedroom, shaking. I grab my black book-bag—the same one I came here with. The one thing that still belongs to me. Then I start collecting my things. The ones I didn't throw away.

A reminder of who I was before him.

CHAPTER TWENTY SIX

GARRET

VERONICA SMACKS me on the arm. "What the hell is the matter with you?"

"What?"

"You don't know?"

I scratch my brow. "You're talking in tongues. First, you fucked up the cake I wanted to surprise her with, and now you're berating me for God knows what." I pick up the plate.

"She's gorgeous," she states. "And very pregnant."

I almost drop the disgusting cake. "What?"

She's been pale for the past couple of days. I count the days. Subtract. Then count again. A slow, proud smile spreads across my lips. She hasn't been eating like she usually does, and she looked at the plate of strawberries like it was covered in mold.

"You think?" I ask, but I already know the answer.

"Yes. And she's also jealous that I'm here." Veronica crosses her arms. "And she knows."

Knows what?

"That we've…" She tilts her head to the side, avoiding the words.

We don't talk about it. It was a mistake, but it happened, and at the time, it helped both of us.

She's happily married and in love with Alaric. And me? I'm in love with the girl who's more than likely pregnant with my child.

"I guess I have to change that."

I wave my hand over the trash. The lid lifts with a soft whir. Reaching in, I pull out the note she threw away. The note where, in not so many words, I told her I love her.

Yeah, I haven't outright said it, but I didn't think I needed to. I was wrong. I was wrong not to introduce her first. And, if I'm being honest with myself, I was an idiot for inviting Veronica in the first place. I didn't think about how she'd feel. I should have.

But I wanted to bake her a cake. To celebrate her birthday. Or at least, the birth date Alaric found for her. It wasn't real—he could only confirm the year, not the month or the day—so I thought of letting her pick one if she wanted.

I didn't want to buy a cake. I didn't know which one to get. I wanted her to taste different flavors and find out which one she loved best. What color she liked. Buttercream icing or whipped? Chocolate, velvet, vanilla, or birthday cake?

But again, I didn't think. I should have never let her walk away. I should have explained. Told her that I love her. That it will always be her.

"What do I do?" I ask, dropping the ruined cake into the trash.

Veronica peers over at the note in my hands, then at me. "What a man should have done a long time ago," she says flatly. "Kill that asshole. Marry her. Create a fucking legacy with her. Fill this house with children of your own."

I smile, imagining a little girl with her smile—Rose wearing my ring.

CHAPTER TWENTY SEVEN

A FLASH OF RED LIGHT. I groan. My head feels like it's being plowed by a bulldozer. One minute, I was walking out of my dorm, putting my things back. The next, I was rushed from behind—something hard slammed against the side of my skull.

Pain throbs behind my left eye as I struggle to peel my eyes open. That damn red light.

The stench in the room makes my stomach twist violently—a foul mix of dirty socks, sweat, sex, and cologne. I gag. Then I vomit. It burns its way up, acid and bile hitting the floor.

"Fucking hell. She threw up again."

David.

His voice is annoyed, disgusted. I inhale through my nose, and my stomach lurches again.

"What the hell is wrong with her?" David asks, irritated. "Is she sick? Did you hit her too hard? She might need a doctor."

No, you piece of shit. I don't need a doctor. I need you to fucking die.

"She's fine," John replies, impatient. "We didn't give her the drugs this time."

John.

John took me. He wasn't supposed to. He broke the rules. But John doesn't give a shit about rules. He's been waiting for this moment. Watching. Plotting. He saw an opportunity, and he took it—like the sick pedophilic fuck he is.

But something isn't right with me. I've felt off since Saturday. I missed my period before I could restart my contraceptive pills. I thought I was safe. I have an IUD. But maybe it failed. And I think I'm pregnant. I won't tell them. It wouldn't save me. I need to be strong.

I pull at my wrists. Nothing. The restraints bite into my skin, tight as ever.

I take a deep breath, swallowing nausea, trying to recognize the scents. John. David. Just the two of them.

I still have the phone Garret gave me. I didn't leave it behind. Just in case. I was right. I can only hope Garret looks for me. If he hasn't given up. Maybe he was waiting for me to leave. Maybe he already got what he wanted. Control.

John curses.

"What's wrong?" David asks.

"The cameras are out."

"Want me to check?"

John exhales sharply. "No. Stay here with her. Clean this shit up."

The door slams. I close my eyes. This is the part David loves. The fact that I'm restrained. The power in forcing me to submit.

He grips my hair. Yanks. Pain splits my skull. The clinking of his belt buckle is unmistakable. And then, the smell. Cinnamon.

I gag.

He rubs cinnamon on the head of his cock. "Stop it and be a good little whore."

I scream.

His hand cracks across my cheek. The burn spreads across my skin, a fire consuming me.

I turn my head away. I inhale deep. He presses closer. I bite. Hard.

The taste of copper explodes in my mouth. David screams.

His hands cup his junk. "You fucking bitch!" he snarls, slapping me again.

Stars explode behind my eyes. I spit in his face. "Fuck… you," I manage, panting.

The door slams open. David freezes. I turn my head. A man in a plague mask stands in the doorway. Dressed in a black long robe.

David starts screaming. My eyes lock on the object in the masked man's gloved hand. John's head. Severed. Dark red muscle and bone hang in shredded tatters.

David chokes. "Who…are you?" His voice shakes with real fear.

The masked man steps forward, the head swinging from his grip.

David glances down, then back up. "She bit my dick," he whimpers. "She bit… I—"

I follow his gaze. John's empty eyes stare at the ceiling. Blood seeps from his ruined skull. Tears leak down my face. I'm going to die. He won't let me live. I know too much.

"Please," David begs. "Let me go. I'll pretend none of this ever happened."

He looks at me. "You can have her. Just let me go."

The man in the mask shakes his head. And lifts John's head like a prize form a hunt. An offering.

David sobs. His hands shake as he cups himself, still bleeding out. "Please…" He holds up the bottle in his hand. "It's cinnamon." Like it's a fucking peace offering. "See?"

The masked man opens his fingers. John's head thuds to the floor. It rolls like a bowling ball.

A long, gleaming knife slips from the man's sleeve. David screams right before the blade swings down. Clean. Precise. David's dick hits the floor. His shrieks shake the walls. He drops to his knees. Tries to grab it. The blade swings again. Vertically. The cut leaves his head in half. Red blood spray paints the walls. David collapses.

The man sheathes the knife.

I lift my chin. I know my fate. This is how I die. I exhale. "If you're going to kill me," I whisper, "make it quick." He pause like he' s listening. Waiting. "And tell Garret…" I swallow hard. My voice drops to a whisper. "That I love him."

I close my eyes. Silence. Then—soft pressure on my wrists. The chains loosen. I wait for the pain. For darkness to drag me under on last time.

I let myself dream. Of a different life. Of Garret. Of our child.

Something cold and damp wipes my lips. The cinnamon is gone. My eyes snap open.

He's there.

Just like in my dreams. The man with the mask. Dressed in black. With no face.

He leans close, his voice soft—so soft, I almost miss it. "I promised I wouldn't let anyone hurt you." His glove drops to the floor as his bare hand presses against my lower belly. His touch is warm, possessive. "This is me saving you, my love." His lips brush my ear. A whisper. A decree. "Welcome to the Order, Mrs. Nox." My eyes widen when he lifts me.

A loud voice cuts through the heavy silence.

"The fuck, Garret? Is she okay?" Melody's voice shakes as she rushes inside, flipping the light to a harsh white. The sudden brightness burns my eyes.

She falls to her knees beside me, her fingers trembling as they brush my face. Her eyes brim with tears, her lips parting in a silent apology. "I'm so sorry…"

She turns to the shadow in the doorway.

"Valen!" she calls out, panic lacing her voice.

A familiar figure steps forward. His voice is calm, but the edge in his tone slices through the air like a blade. "He has her, Melody. Chill."

ABOUT THE AUTHOR

Carmen Rosales is a best-selling Dark Romance and Latinx author. She loves to write in different genres of Romance and erotic horror under her alter ego, Delilah Croww. Beyond her writing, Carmen is a devoted wife and mother who loves spending time with her loved ones. Join her VIP list at www.carmenrosales.com

Join her VIP list- www.carmenrosales.com

.

Scan the QR code to follow her on Social Media, sign up for her Newsletter, and for preorder links for upcoming releases: